THE COMMODORE'S CUP

The Black Buccaneer
Down the Big River
Longshanks
Red Horse Hill
Away to Sea
King of the Hills
Lumberjack
The Will to Win and Other Stories
Who Rides in the Dark?
T-Model Tommy
Bat: The Story of a Bull Terrier
Boy with a Pack
Clear for Action!
Blueberry Mountain
Shadow in the Pines
The Sea Snake
The Long Trains Roll
Skippy's Family
Jonathan Goes West
Behind the Ranges
River of the Wolves
Cedar's Boy
Whaler 'Round the Horn
Bulldozer
The Fish Hawk's Nest
Sparkplug of the Hornets
The Buckboard Stranger
Guns for the Saratoga
Sabre Pilot
Everglades Adventure

THE COMMODORE'S CUP

STEPHEN W. MEADER

Illustrated by Don Sibley

SOUTHERN SKIES

SOUTHERN SKIES

LITTLE ROCK, ARKANSAS

www.southernskies.com

Dedication

The republication of this book is dedicated with love to Charlton Buckley---business genius, collector, trusted friend, sweet soul---by Jerry Atchley

THE COMMODORE'S CUP

1

Labor Day morning dawned gray and foggy. Up before seven, Luke Cramer hurried outside to look at the weather-vane and sniff the wind. Such air as there was came from the southwest. That meant the mist would blow off by mid-morning and there ought to be a fair sailing breeze when the races started.

All of his nearly seventeen years Luke had lived on Man-o'-War Island. He remembered a lot of Labor Days but none quite like this one. All through the weekend, cars had been pouring across the causeway, bringing perhaps a hundred thousand extra people to crowd the twenty-mile strip of sand that stretched along the New Jersey coast between Man-o'-War Bay and the sea.

This was a special Labor Day for Luke. He was going to crew for Bruce Canning in the final Comet Class race of the season—the Man-o'-War Yacht Club Invitation. Half the youngsters on the island would have given their eye teeth to be in his place.

Breakfast wouldn't be ready for another half hour, and Luke decided he had time to get over to the Yacht Club and make sure the *Sally C* was all right. With his black Labrador, Bunkie, running beside him, he rode his bicycle south on the highway and down the gravel road leading to the bay. First he saw the forest of slim masts, then the shining hulls of the Comets, perched in a long row on their trailers by the landing. License plates on those trailers bore the names of half a dozen states. This race had brought sailors from New York and Pennsylvania, Delaware, and Maryland. The home-breds would have a tough job on their hands.

Luke located the *Sally C* and stood there, thrilled as always by her clean lines. He ran his hand along the satin-smooth paint on her deck and sides and bottom. He knew something about the days and weeks of hard labor that went into a racing finish. After a few minutes the early sun broke through the mist and glinted on stainless steel stays, shrouds, and spreaders. He took a chamois from the bow cuddy and carefully wiped away the dew that had settled on the deck and the brightwork. Then, with a last fond look at the little sloop, he hurried up the road again toward home.

The Cramers had a comfortable two-story house on the main highway that ran down the middle of the island. Unlike most of the summer cottages, it was heated and equipped for year-round living. In winter the half-dozen townships strung along the coastal dunes held only two or three thousand people—fishermen, clam-diggers, and a few local businessmen. Seth Cramer, Luke's father, owned the hardware store in the village of Cedar Cove. During nine months of the year his business hardly paid taxes. From June to September was the time when the year's income had to be made, and he kept three clerks busy, with occasional help from the family.

Luke and his twelve-year-old sister Joan attended Man-o'-War Regional School in Marshtown, on the mainland, across the bay. All too soon they would be going back there, riding the big yellow school buses.

For two hundred years there had been Cramers living on that part of the Jersey coast. The name was spelled in

8

various ways—Cramer, Crammer, or Cranmer—but all the family sprang from the same English stock. Luke was proud of his seagoing heritage. In the Revolution an ancestor of his named Eliphalet Cramer had commanded a privateer that captured nearly a dozen British prizes.

Man-o'-War Island itself had a long and colorful history. It had seen scores of shipwrecks and several naval battles. Buccaneers had careened their vessels there and possibly—according to local legend—had buried some of their treasure in the cedar-covered dunes. Smugglers had landed their contraband cargoes on the long, lonely beaches. Even the names of places held a hint of nautical romance.

There was Foremast Haven, at the southernmost tip, and Mizzen Inlet, far to the north. Cannon Beach was so called because of the guns that had once been hauled ashore there from a wrecked frigate. And the town of Long Tom got its name from another cannon—a big one—set up in the dunes to defend the coast in the War of 1812.

Only three of the family sat down to breakfast. Seth Cramer was sleeping late on the holiday, for the store would be closed.

"Well," said Joanie, sipping her orange juice, "was that precious boat still there?"

Luke smiled at the tart remark. "No need to be jealous, small fry," he told her. "Some day you'll have a chance to crew a Comet, when you get big enough. Maybe I'll have one o' my own by then."

"Hmph!" She tossed her head. "Any time you get a real racing boat you'll probably be middle-aged, with gray whiskers. I expect some sailor'll want my help long before that."

"Listen, you two," said Mrs. Cramer mildly, "let's not have any spats this early in the day. I want your father to get some sleep. How'll you have your eggs, Luke—flipped or sunny side up?"

An hour afterward the boy was down at the landing again. The Lightnings, with their three-man crews, were already in the water. They were scheduled to race first, at eleven-fifty. Then the Comets would start at noon, and ten minutes later the little single-sailed Moths would get under way.

Mr. Canning arrived shortly, and as he got out of his car, Luke gave him a smart salute. "All shipshape, sir," he told his skipper. "Looks like a southwest breeze. By starting time I reckon it'll pick up a bit."

Canning was a tall, curly-haired man of thirty, who ran a successful real estate business on the island. He glanced up at the turkey feather atop the mast and nodded.

"Wind's in the right direction if it doesn't shift," he agreed. "They've laid out a six-mile course today, twice around. We'll have a reach north to the first marker, then a westward beat for about a mile into Dutchman's Bay. When we turn the marker there, we run back before the wind to the north buoy again, and come about for what could be one long tack to the starting line. Think you can handle that jib real fast today?"

"I'll sure try!" Luke answered fervently. "You want to get the sails on her now?"

"No hurry," Canning said, smiling. "Let's go over the standing rigging first—make sure everything's in order."

They tested each turnbuckle and clamp, oiled the big wooden pulley that raised and lowered the bronze center-board, checked out the hiking straps, the rudder, and all the chocks and sheaves.

When Canning was satisfied, he went to the trunk of his car and carefully lifted out the folded nylon sails. The foot of the mainsail was packed on top, so that it was ready to be threaded into a slot that ran the length of the boom. Sewed into the lower edge of the sail was the bolt rope—a stout quarter-inch manila line with a smaller cord attached to its after end. Starting next to the mast, Canning worked the foot of the sail into the circular tunnel in the boom, pulling the bolt rope aft by the cord that protruded from the slot on top. When the foot of the sail was hauled out nearly to the end of the boom, they turned their attention to the luff—the leading edge of the triangular mainsail. Luke started placing the stainless steel slides on the track that ran all the way up the mast. With the sail hoisted to about half its height, Canning took the three thin slats of wood called battens and put them into their pockets in the leech—the after edge of the sail.

The jib was a simpler matter. That could wait till the boat was in the water.

"Well," the skipper said, "it's nine-thirty and the strangers will be cluttering up the bay pretty soon. Let's make a trial run around the course."

They backed the light trailer down the ramp and Luke jumped into the shallow water to steady the *Sally C.* As soon as she floated, they hauled her sails aloft, tightened the stays, and a few minutes later were tacking out from the landing.

Canning kept an eye on the set of the mainsail at the head, and took up on the outhaul a bit till the wrinkles disappeared. Both sheet ropes were within reach of his hand. He looked aloft at the tell-tale, found the light breeze steady and trimmed the main sheet till the little craft was pointed well up, heeled to starboard on the port tack. They cut smoothly through the water. Luke hooked his bare feet under a hiking strap and sat high on the port gunwale.

"Ready to come about," said Canning, and the boy ducked low under the boom as he felt the helm go over.

Out in front of the Yacht Club the fleet was already assembling, and there were three or four Comets testing the course like themselves. They practiced a couple of starts in the busy traffic, then bore away on the northward reach with the wind over their port quarter. It was blowing a bit stronger now, and the *Sally C* made good time to the first marker. There she came about smartly and started beating westward. Dutchman's Bay was only about three hundred yards wide, so it was necessary to tack often.

"Here's where the smart sailors will pull ahead," the skipper told Luke. "We'll have to keep our eyes open or we'll be jockeyed out of position. How's the tide right now?"

"Just past low," said Luke. "By noon it'll be flowing in fast. Are you wondering about that little inside channel?"

Canning nodded. "Some of the local boats may try it if they think they've got enough water. The others probably won't dare. The course rules don't bar it though."

When they turned the buoy in Dutchman's Bay, Luke sprang forward and set the whisker pole at the clew of the jib. The little sloop sped before the wind, her mainsail to port and her jib to starboard—"wung out" as the phrase went.

"Look alive, son," Canning warned as they swept down on the northern marker. "I'm going to jibe the turn."

It was a pretty maneuver. Just as they came abreast of the buoy, he trimmed the mainsail amidships, and at the same instant Luke snatched out the whisker pole, letting the jib flap. In a matter of seconds the boat had swung neatly about, turning the buoy and pointing west on the port tack. The moment she had full headway again Canning put her over, with the wind from starboard.

"Now," he said, "we'll see if we can fetch the finish on this tack."

He kept her pointed high and she held the course with

very little drift. Ahead of them, down channel, they could see twenty or thirty other boats maneuvering. Canning bore off to keep clear of them and took the sloop into the mooring basin just behind the Yacht Club. There, in the lee of a long dock, they found a place to tie up in the line of Comets already in the water. Others were being launched. The whole area buzzed with activity as crews hailed one another and skippers made last-minute changes in their rig.

Canning came forward and followed Luke onto the dock. He gave the boy a clap on the shoulder. "See you here at eleven-thirty sharp," he said. "The boat's right. If she doesn't finish with the leaders, we'll be to blame."

*   *   *

The five-minute gun sounded and the blue flag went up, as the starter's voice blared out over the public address system. The *Sally C* was headed south on the port tack, a quarter mile down the bay from the line.

Canning checked his waterproof wrist watch. "We'll go down a bit farther," he said, "and come back with the wind. There's no hurry. That breeze is getting stronger and it's swung south, so we'll have to plan a different race from the trial we sailed."

Four other Comets were ahead of them as they tacked southward, away from the starting line, and others followed. A lot of skippers seemed to have the same idea. There was some luffing and falling off to avoid collisions as they neared the south buoy, and Canning deliberately sheered off, letting the other boats get out of the way. At the two-minute announcement he looked at his watch again, then came about with the wind right astern.

To Luke those final moments seemed to drag endlessly. All the rest of the boats were ahead of them and he sat tense, silently urging the *Sally C* on, sure they would be left behind. But Canning knew what he was about. He held the helm steady, heading across the course toward the side of the line nearest the clubhouse. Again he glanced at his watch.

As they came close, Luke could hear him whispering the count-down. "Seven seconds—six seconds—five—"

Then the whisper was lost in the confusion of the start. Boats that had edged over the line too soon were frantically clawing their way back. Others drifted, bows to the wind, ready to fill away. And still others tacked back and forth by the outer mark, their skippers yelling exasperated warnings at each other. Canning had timed his approach perfectly. The nose of the Comet was almost on the line when the red signal flag went up and the gun sounded.

"Up for'ard, Luke!" he shouted. "Snap that jib over and set the pole. We'll run wing-and-wing."

The boy complied in a matter of seconds, then scuttled aft as close to the helmsman as he could get. He knew the boat would plane, once their weight brought the bow out. The breeze continued to freshen, and sure enough the *Sally C* lifted her forefoot and skimmed along on the after part of her hull. Luke needed no signal from Canning to haul the centerboard up.

They had been first over the line and still held the lead, although three other boats were close behind. Luke could identify two of them. One—the nearest—was painted a light, bright green and the boy at her helm was a burly seventeen-year-old with a blond crew cut. That was Mert Holliger, Jr., the richest kid in the island's summer colony, and his boat was the *Haulfast*. Another bore the number 3001 on her sail, and he knew she was the *Gull*, owned by Marley Evans, who had introduced Comet racing on the bay. The third he didn't recognize—probably a boat from Long Island or the Delaware.

Holliger had been clear over at the outside marker at

the start and was making a broad reach of it, footing a little faster than the *Sally C*, but sailing a somewhat longer course. Both had their booms over the port side, so the right of way would belong to the sloop that had the lead when they neared the northern mark.

The green boat pulled even as their courses converged. With a quarter mile to go, Holliger grinned over at Luke and brought his helm up to cross their bows. Canning was unperturbed. He dropped the centerboard, shifted the tiller a bit, and no sooner had the *Haulfast* passed in front of them than she was blanketed by the *Sally C's* sails. As the green boat lost way, Canning brought the helm up once more and cut smartly past his rival, still "wung-out," still heading for the buoy.

Meanwhile the other two leading craft had gained. Evans, only a couple of lengths astern, was almost neck-and-neck with the out-of-state Comet. And all four were sweeping down on the marker at top speed.

Canning's voice crackled through the sound of wind and waves. "Get for'ard," he ordered. "I'm going to cut the buoy close. Be ready to jibe."

The *Sally C* had the inside track and was three or four yards ahead of the *Haulfast*, now rushing in on the port tack.

"Give way!" Holliger shouted. "Can't you see I'll hit you?"

Canning didn't answer. It would be close, Luke saw, but he knew they had the right of way. They shot past the marker and at the same instant Canning hauled the main sheet, bringing the boom amidships. Luke had freed the jib. The sloop heeled gracefully to starboard, clearing the buoy with a yard or two to spare. With no room to cut inside, the green Comet had had to fall off.

Mert Holliger's face was crimson. "I'll get you for that," he yelled, and shook his fist after them as the *Sally C* scudded away on the reach into Dutchman's Bay.

2

The four leading boats were still close-bunched when they neared the western marker. Looking over his shoulder, Luke could see the rest of the fleet strung out along a mile of the course, and some, after a slow start, were still trying to round the north buoy.

The *Sally C* was sailing well, but she no longer held an unchallenged lead. The *Gull* was right behind her and the stranger had worked up through their lee to forge slightly ahead. The name on her transom was visible now. She was the *Go-Devil* from New York—a fast sloop that had often been mentioned in the papers that summer. The man at her helm was handling her like a master.

At the west buoy the turn had to be made from the starboard side, coming into the wind and rounding the marker counter-clockwise. It was no surprise to the *Sally C's* crew that the New York boat should try to luff them out of position. As she crowded closer, Canning put his helm down enough to keep clear, but after a moment he suddenly slacked the sheet, brought the helm hard up and cut to starboard, just missing the stern of the *Go-Devil.*

The maneuver caught his opponent still luffing. Before he could fall off, the *Sally C* was through his lee, footing fast for the yellow-flagged buoy. Luke held back a cheer. He was proud of his skipper.

They rounded the marker a boat's length ahead, with Evans and Holliger hanging tight in third and fourth places. Now the flooding tide was against them. Perched high on the starboard gunwale, Luke got a feeling of tremendous speed from the racing waves. Yet he could see by looking at the reeds along the shore that they were really making slow progress.

"Luke," said Canning, "you know this bay pretty well. Which side does the current run strongest?"

"I'd say the middle and the north side," Luke answered. "Ought to be slack over to starboard."

The skipper nodded and pointed higher into the wind, cutting across in front of the westbound pack. Behind him Luke could see Marley Evans perform the same maneuver, but the *Go-Devil* and the *Haulfast* held stubbornly to their course.

Who was right? It took three or four minutes to make sure, but by the time they cleared the point at the entrance to the cove there was no question about it. The *Sally C* had five good lengths over the New York boat, and Evans was now solidly in second place.

There was something of a traffic jam at the northern buoy, for stragglers were still coming around it, headed west. But the rules of the day called for all turns to be made counter-clockwise. That meant the *Sally C* had to go in to windward, making a complete circle around the marker.

One of the slower Comets was nearing the buoy as they approached. She was awkwardly handled and Canning was forced to put his helm down and wait his turn. Evans, just far enough astern to avoid the tangle, seized his opportunity. Cutting close to the buoy he came smartly about inside the other boat and had a two-length lead by the time Canning got around. The *Go-Devil* and the *Haul-*

fast gained as well, and Luke's heart sank as he saw the New York boat surging right alongside.

Canning took it philosophically. "Bad break," he said. "But you've got to expect a few. This beat to windward may give us another chance."

Close-bunched, the other three sloops were all on the port tack, heading over toward the westward side of the channel.

"Ready to come about," said the skipper sharply, and as the boom swung over, the *Sally C* sped straight down channel on the starboard tack.

Luke glanced at the tell-tale on the masthead and realized that the wind had shifted a point or two to the west. The others would discover it soon enough, but there was a momentary advantage—maybe even a chance to regain the lead.

Close-hauled, the *Sally C* was footing fast despite the tide, heeled over till the waves creamed above her gunwale. Luke lay back with his body far out over the weather side, feet secured in the hiking strap. The other three Comets had come about now. He could see Evans in the lead, closely followed by the green boat and the New Yorker. It was hard to say how much the *Sally C* had gained, but Luke thought her bow was about even with the leader's when they clawed past the clubhouse.

"Too bad," said Canning. "Can't quite make it on this leg. Here we go about."

Once again they were favored by a flaw in the wind. Hardly had they tacked when it shifted southward again. Marveling, Luke wondered if his skipper had seen it coming. At the moment, however, he had something else to think about. The three other boats, all on the starboard tack, were rapidly converging on their own course. There was no question about their rivals having the right of way.

The *Sally C* must either luff or fall off and go astern of them.

Canning took the latter choice. He slacked the sheet for the few seconds needed, then pointed up again, heading toward the starboard side of the south buoy. The other sloops had been so intent on cutting across his bows that none had noticed the shift of wind. Now they took action. Evans was the first to come about, followed quickly by the two who trailed him. By the time they had full headway the *Sally C* was almost even with the leader and in a good leeward position.

There was a real scramble at the marker. Evans rounded first, with the *Go-Devil* and the *Sally C* just outside him. Sailing recklessly, Holliger cut inside so close that his weather gunwale actually scraped the buoy.

"Ha, ha!" he shouted at Luke. "I said I'd get ya!"

There was a judges' boat a hundred feet away. "Three-oh-nine-five!" bellowed a voice through the megaphone. "You're penalized for striking the marker! Fall off and come around again or I'll disqualify you!"

What the young skipper of the green boat said was lost in the wind, but it must have been sulphurous. Luke caught a glimpse of his black scowl as the *Sally C* rounded and he spread the jib wing-and-wing for the run up channel. For a while, at least, they had only two opponents to worry about.

A scant two lengths separated all three leaders as they made for the north buoy on the second lap. If anything, the *Sally C* gained a trifle on the next leg, crosswind to the westward, and she was even with the New York boat when they squared away for the eastward reach out of Dutchman's Bay. Luke wondered where Holliger was, and leaned forward to peer between the mast and the leech of the jib. It was lucky he did.

"Look out!" he yelled to Canning. Tearing down on the

21

opposite course toward the west buoy, the green Comet suddenly bore over as if she meant to run them down. Only by fast work at sheet and helm was Canning able to sheer off.

"What's wrong with that kid?" he asked angrily. "Is he crazy?"

"Sort of," Luke replied. "Anyhow, he sure hates to get licked."

They passed the entrance to the little short-cut channel through the marsh. It would have saved them fifty yards or more, but with the tide at only half flood it would be dangerous. Evans apparently thought so too, for he kept the *Gull* in the main bay.

Mert Holliger had no such qualms. He had turned the buoy a dozen lengths astern. Now Luke saw him steer recklessly into the cut. He must have raised his centerboard, for his crew man was fending off the lee bank with an oar.

"If he gets stuck," Canning grinned, "it'll serve him dead right."

But by luck or a miracle the *Haulfast* came through. She was less than three lengths back when they rounded the north marker for the final leg of the race.

The next few minutes were among the most exciting Luke had ever known. It was still possible for any of the first four boats to win. The breeze held steady from the south and it was a question of which Comet could move fastest to windward and which crew came about most smartly.

The *Gull* and the *Sally C* were on the port tack, almost together, with the *Go-Devil* right behind them. Holliger chose the starboard tack and it was hard to tell whether he would lose or gain by it. The excitement had spread to the spectators. They could hear distant yells of encouragement from the clubhouse dock, borne toward them by the wind. The broad channel ahead was cluttered with dozens of speedboats and cruisers, hurrying into position to watch the finish.

"Ought to make it in three tacks," said Canning. "I'm going about pretty quick. Get ready."

Theirs was the first of the trio to tack. Evans, on their lee, came over seconds later, and the New York boat followed. As they crossed in front of the *Haulfast*, Luke could see she was a hundred feet astern. Only one break could save Holliger now—a flaw in the wind. It was what he had played for, and what he got.

Suddenly the *Sally C's* sails flapped. The breeze had shifted southeast without warning.

"Quick!" yelled Canning. "Got to tack before we lose way!"

He jerked the boom over and jammed down the helm. After a moment's faltering the gallant little sloop heeled to starboard and began footing fast again.

They were ahead and to leeward of the *Gull* and the *Go-Devil*. Much farther to leeward, and almost even now, was the green boat. And the markers of the finish line in front of the clubhouse rocked in the channel less than a quarter of a mile away.

"We've got it!" Luke told himself exultantly. "We don't have to point as high as Holliger, and we'll make more speed!"

Then occurred one of those unfortunate breaks that sometimes happen in sailing races. A thirty-foot cruiser roared past on the east side of the channel. They saw her big bow wave surging at them, three or four feet high. Hiked far out on the windward gunwale, Luke hung on as best he could while the wave tossed the sloop over almost on her side. Only Canning's smart seamanship kept her from capsizing. By the time she was righted half her mainsail was wet.

The *Gull*, unharmed, scudded past them with the *Go-Devil* close at her heels. Canning's face was grim. "That lost us the race," he growled, "but by thunder we can still give the *Haulfast* a licking. Did you notice whose motorboat that was?"

Luke shook his head. "I was too busy trying to stay aboard. Why?"

"The owner's Merton Holliger, Senior," said Canning. He trimmed the wet sail skillfully and they struggled on toward the finish. From the Yacht Club a voice came over the P.A. system.

"You're over, three-oh-oh-one," it said. "Nice win, Marley!"

Then, seconds later: "Three-one-nine-oh—over! Well sailed, *Go-Devil*."

The roar of the crowd mounted in volume as the fight for third place reached a climax. At the last moment young Holliger realized he was too far to leeward to get inside the buoy without coming about. He tacked in a hurry, but by then it was too late.

"Three-one-oh-three—over!" boomed the announcer. "A fine try, Bruce, and tough luck."

They sailed into the Yacht Club basin. "You aim to file a protest, Mr. Canning?" Luke asked.

"It doesn't mean that much to me," the skipper said. "If it was done on purpose, to give the *Haulfast* the race, it didn't work. Anyhow the Race Committee saw what happened. I expect they'll post tighter rules for power craft on the course. But old Holliger won't be called on the carpet. He's too important here on the island."

Luke knew what he meant. Merton Holliger owned the biggest house and the biggest swimming pool on Man-o'-War. He dominated Yacht Club politics, too. Said to be a millionaire several times over, he was the principal owner of a famous trucking company, and his giant trailers, painted pea-green with the name "Holliger Haulfast Truck Lines" in big white letters, rolled along the roads from Florida to New England and as far west as Cleveland.

Everybody knew Merton Junior was a badly spoiled boy. He had more spending money than was good for him. He flogged a Cadillac convertible up and down the island at hair-raising speeds, and on the rare occasions when a local constable picked him up he was promptly freed by his father. He wasn't a bad sailor, for he had owned boats since he was ten. But his lack of respect for racing rules was notorious.

Carefully they took down the *Sally C's* sails and spread the mainsail to dry in the sun. There was little conversation until the sloop had been hauled out on her trailer. Then Bruce Canning grinned at Luke. "We had a pretty good day, at that," he said. "Third in a good field isn't anything to be ashamed of. And I couldn't have asked for a better crew man."

He put out a big brown hand and Luke shook it proudly. As he went up to the clubhouse porch to watch the Moths finish, he was whistling. There'd be other Labor Days, he told himself, and other races.

3

Two days later, brushed and scrubbed, and in their school clothes, the two young Cramers went out to the corner of the main highway to wait for the bus. Joan was happy. She would be starting high school and, even more important, she was wearing a new dress. To Luke, who was an outdoor kind of boy, the thought of school had less appeal. He did well enough in his studies and he knew he wanted a good education, but he was going to miss the excitement of racing weekends.

Aboard the bus, several of his friends were waiting for him. He sat down beside Johnny Grasso, whose father had the shoe repair shop in Long Tom village. The Italian boy's black eyes were shining.

"Some race that was on Labor Day," he said, grinning. "Thought you were goin' to win it, there at the end. Sure was a tough piece o' luck—if you can call it that."

"You saw what happened?" Luke asked him. "Where were you?"

"Right out at the end o' the Yacht Club dock. I heard one o' the judges say that fool girl ought to be ruled off the course."

"Girl?" asked Luke, surprised. "What girl?"

"Why that Marilyn March that runs around with Mert Holliger. You know—the cute blonde from Pittsburgh. She and a couple of other chicks were out watchin' the race in the Holliger boat. Her father's a big shot in the trucking outfit—vice president in charge o' the western division."

Luke nodded. The cruiser had gone by so fast he hadn't seen who was at the wheel, but he knew the girl Johnny meant—tanned and yellow-haired and beautiful. He had sometimes seen her sailing as crew in the *Haulfast*.

"Well," he said, "what did the other judges say?"

"One of 'em had been lookin' the other way when that bow wave hit you. The other said he thought it was just— what was it he called it?—'careless high spirits.' "

Luke laughed. "Didn't look careless to me," he said. "It was a slick piece o' work. Only thing she did wrong was to miss swamping Marley Evans and that New York boat. If she'd got all three of us, it would have fixed things up for Mert just dandy."

"You weren't around the clubhouse afterward, were you?" Johnny asked. "There was quite a scene when the Holligers came in. Mert wanted to claim you fouled him at the north buoy, and o' course his old man backed him up. The Race Committee refused it, though, an' Mr. Holliger really got hot. He said okay, he'd get his son a new boat that would sail circles around anything on the bay, an' next year we'd see who won the Commodore's Cup."

"That ought to be interesting," Luke said, with a chuckle. "What's she going to have—a secret outboard motor? Far as I know, Comets are all about as fast as the designers can make 'em, and they're all one class. It's the way they're sailed that counts in a race."

School started and Luke quickly adjusted himself to the new routine. Homework was tougher this year, but there were other things to make up for it. The summer people were nearly all gone now, and the island and the bay were more the way he liked them. Actually, September was the best month of the year. It was still warm and

27

sunny without being too hot, and the surf stayed warm enough for swimming.

Many of the Comets were gone—either hauled up for the winter in the boat yards or hauled away by their owners. But Luke could still do some sailing of a kind. His three most precious possessions were the big black dog, Bunkie, his twelve-gauge shotgun, and his sneakbox. The last was a small, shallow-draft boat, very low in the water, that could be rowed or paddled in among the reeds in duck season. It could also be sailed, when it was fitted with a mast and leeboards.

On a Saturday morning in mid-September he ran up the leg-o'-mutton sail on the little ten-foot craft and steered out from his own landing. Bunkie lay comfortably on the narrow deck to windward, his tail wagging and his amber eyes watching the boom. Weighing close to ninety pounds, he made excellent ballast, and he shifted sides smartly when the boat came about.

There was a steady wind from the south. Luke tacked out across the blue emptiness of the bay with the little boat footing nicely through the waves. The leeboards weren't very efficient at keeping her from drifting and she wouldn't point very close to the wind, but he was going nowhere in particular and didn't care. The main fun of sailing was to keep the feel of the boat through sheet and tiller, to study the currents in different parts of the bay, and to learn how to use them to advantage.

He knew, for instance, that the tide ran faster in the main channel than in the shallower water along the shores. It was coming in now. Wind and current were both against him, and a glance at the landmarks told him he was doing little more than holding his own. He cut well over toward the west bank till he reached slack water, then brought the sneakbox around on the starboard tack.

As he headed southeastward, the sun was in his eyes

and he half closed them, lolling back on the cockpit coaming. The solitude was something he enjoyed—nobody around but Bunkie and himself and the mewing, circling gulls.

Then the silence was broken by the distant thunder of an engine. Two miles to the south he saw the flash of sun on a white bow wave.

"Shucks!" he told the dog with a grin. "We're not as lonesome as we thought. Wonder whose boat that is. She's sure making knots."

He started to tack again, then thought better of it. Any boat under sail had the right of way, and on the course the big power-cruiser was making there was no danger of a collision. Besides, he would rather take her wake head on. She was only a quarter of a mile away now and coming like a locomotive. Suddenly the big craft swung toward him.

"Hey!" he yelled at the top of his lungs, but the roar of the engine drowned his voice. There was a desperate instant when it seemed the sharp mahogany prow would cut the little sailboat right in two. Then it veered again. Above him, only a few feet away, Luke saw two faces. One, contorted with laughter, was Mert Holliger's. The other was a girl's, wide-eyed and scared. Then he saw no more, for the shock of the huge wave tossed him into the bay.

He came up for air and found Bunkie swimming strongly beside him. The capsized sneakbox was a dozen yards away, floating on its side, the mast and sail in the water.

Luke had neither time nor breath to voice his wrath. The water was cold and he had a job to do.

"Okay, boy," he told the dog through chattering teeth, "get over there and do your stuff."

It was a trick they had practiced before. The big Labrador swam to the far side of the hull and scrambled up till his forepaws gripped the gunwale. Luke, meanwhile, got

hold of the mast and the floating sail. With a quick tug he pulled the mast out of its step, and the dog's weight righted the boat.

For the next ten minutes Luke was busy bailing. At last he had all but a few gallons of water out of the hull, and he pulled the mast and dripping sail aboard. Luckily the short oar he kept stowed forward had not floated off. Slowly he was able to paddle back across the current to the dock. Just as he reached it, the big motor boat came down the channel again, this time at half speed. Holliger must have run all the way up to Mizzen Inlet and back.

The cruiser was too far out for Luke to see the faces of the pair in it, but he was pretty sure the boy at the wheel waved at him mockingly. The fact that they might have drowned him seemed to bother Mert Holliger not at all.

Luke tipped the boat over to run the last of the water out and spread the sail to dry. The simple rigging was tangled but intact. One of the leeboards showed a crack that would need mending. Otherwise the only damage was to Luke's feelings. As he sat in the sun, drying his clothes, he considered what he could do about it. If he told the local constable or even the state police that the other boy had deliberately capsized him, the chances were they wouldn't believe it. And there were no witnesses. As far as he knew, not a single soul on shore had been in a position to see what happened. He clenched his fist, wishing he could drive it into the middle of that hatefully grinning face.

After a while his T-shirt, dungarees, and sneakers had pretty well dried out. He got to his feet, snapped his fingers for Bunkie to follow him, and started up the sandy road toward home. As he neared the main north-south highway, a white Thunderbird rolled slowly to a stop right in front of him. Its top was down and there was only one person in it—a girl. Her blond hair was wind-blown and her pretty, tanned face was troubled.

"You're Luke Cramer, aren't you?" she said. "I'm Marilyn March, and I came up here to tell you something."

"Okay," said Luke gruffly, "go ahead."

She flushed, hesitating over the difficult words. "I'm sorry," she said. "Sorry and ashamed. I've known Mert Holliger quite a while, but I never realized until this morning what a heel he is. That was a mean thing he did, and dangerous. You might have been—killed!"

Looking at her, Luke realized she was close to tears.

"Aw, forget it," he told her. "I know you weren't to blame. But you can tell Mert that any time he's ready for a fair contest—a race or a fight or anything he wants—I'd like to take him on."

She nodded but she still looked unhappy. "I doubt if I'll be seeing that big ape again," she said. "Not if I can help it, anyway. I go back to school tomorrow and he'll be leaving in a day or two. I wanted to tell you something else. At the end of the race on Labor Day I got the crazy notion I could help him win if I stirred up the water a little. He didn't put me up to it. It was my own sappy idea and I've felt rotten about it ever since. I'm here to apologize—if that does any good."

Luke's sober face broke into a grin and he took the hand she held out to him.

"Sure," he said. "Hearing you say it helps a lot. Sorry you're leaving so soon. I'd like to have met you earlier."

"That goes double," she smiled. "But there's still tonight. There's a pretty good movie at the Buccaneer—or have you already seen it?"

❈　　❈　　❈

All Luke's anger had evaporated, he realized, when he was brushing his best sports jacket after supper. "Marilyn."

He'd always thought it a silly name before, but now it had a lovely sound. He borrowed the family car—a respectable last year's Buick sedan—and drove down the island. He knew where the girl lived, in the swank section of Foremast Haven. She was there, waiting for him.

It was, as she had said, a pretty good movie, and it was about the sea. Some of the storm photography was so powerful and so grim that Luke held his breath. Marilyn must have been stirred by it, too, for her hand stole over and clutched his.

"Wow!" she said with a shiver when they came out. "A little more of that and I'd have been seasick. But I loved it."

He took her to Wrecker's Roost, a favorite teen-age haunt where they sat on stools, absorbed giant frosted shakes, and got better acquainted. Although her home was in a suburb of Pittsburgh, she went to a well-known girls' school on the Philadelphia Main Line. Luke found her natural and friendly.

"You know, Luke," she told him, "you ought to have a Comet of your own. I expect you're a good sailor."

"I'm trying to learn," he said. "And Bruce Canning's a mighty good teacher. But I've got a way to go yet. Besides, a decent second-hand boat costs more'n I could afford. Three or four hundred dollars for the hull and spars. Another couple of hundred for a good suit of sails and rigging. I suppose that must sound like pin money to you, though."

She chuckled. "Don't you believe it! I'm not the spoiled-rich type. Dad and Mother are a lot smarter that way than some parents I could name. All I get is a small monthly allowance. That white T-bird isn't mine. It's Mom's—an anniversary present she got last June. Some day, though, when I'm out of college and earning my own money, I'd like to have a boat down here. And since I won't be seeing so much of Mert Holliger, maybe *you* could teach me to sail before then."

"Golly," said he, "you mean it? There's nothing I'd like better."

All in all, the evening was a great success. Luke drove home in a rosy glow. The next day he waited a full hour by the side of the highway for a chance glimpse of the departing March family. At last, just as he was about to give up, he saw their chauffeur-driven Lincoln go by. Then came the Thunderbird, with Mrs. March at the wheel and Marilyn beside her. She was looking the other way, talking to her mother. But she turned her head just as they passed, saw him, and waved.

Luke's sister was sitting on the steps when he got home, wearing her bathing suit.

"Boy!" she remarked. "Have you got it bad! I've been waiting I don't know how long for you to go swimming. Get your trunks on and I'll see you at the beach."

4

For the next few weeks Luke was filled with one idea—to get enough money together to buy some kind of sailboat, no matter how old and decrepit it might be. He teased his father into letting him clerk at the store evenings, even though business was beginning to be slack. Saturdays he spent around the boat yards, picking up a few dollars helping to haul out boats. At the same time he kept an eye out for bargains.

The only boats up for sale were clumsily designed, damaged and battered, or weakened by dry rot. And even these were priced far beyond his present means. By early October, in spite of all his work and scrimping, he could count only ninety-five dollars and a few cents. Meanwhile his chances to earn more were rapidly running out.

His spirits were raised for a day or two by a letter from Marilyn. It wasn't a very long one but the fact that she had written at all made him happy. He replied at once. After that the correspondence lagged. The better part of a month went by before he heard from her again.

The weather was remarkable that fall. Day after sunny day went by and the temperature stayed almost as warm as summer. It was late in October before the change came. Luke heard the warning first, for he had the radio on as usual while he did his homework.

"We interrupt this program," said the announcer, "to bring you the latest report from the Miami Weather Station. A rapidly moving tropical storm center has formed east of the Virgin Islands and appears headed toward the mainland. Winds of gale force are reported from Puerto Rico. Hurricane-hunting planes over the area say the most peculiar characteristic of this storm is its fast forward motion—forty to fifty miles an hour. As yet no warnings have been posted north of Jacksonville, but coastwise vessels are alerted for possible trouble."

By morning the storm had a name. It was called Greta and it had developed into a compact, fast-traveling hurricane with winds as high as ninety miles an hour. It would almost certainly miss the Florida coast, forecasters said, but was likely to cause some damage in North Carolina. Storm warnings were up from Cape Hatteras to Block Island.

Luke looked out at the overcast sky. The wind was moaning in off the sea—not strongly yet but in brief gusts that might be a foretaste of bigger winds to come. The boy went to the barometer on the wall of the living room. The red needle had moved down from thirty, where it had stood for days, to twenty-nine and six-tenths. That was a four-point drop in twelve hours—rapid but not too alarming.

A fine rain had begun to spit when it was time for the school bus. At his mother's insistence Luke took his slicker. Joan, who had a cold, was kept at home. As he rode across the long causeway to the mainland, Luke watched the choppy waves starting to kick up whitecaps on the bay. He was sitting up front and saw the driver shake his head dubiously.

"Dunno's they'll keep school all day," he remarked. He was an old bayman who dug clams and sold bait in the summer.

36

"Moon's right for a big spring tide," he continued. "If the wind comes on to blow real strong an' backs it up in the bay, we might have water pretty near over the road here by sundown."

Classes at Man-o'-War Regional High didn't go very well that day. The students were fidgety, watching the rain dash against the windows and listening to the roar of the rising wind. Even some of the teachers had a hard time keeping their minds on their work.

Shortly after the noon recess the principal came to the door of Luke's room and said a few words to the instructor. Then it was announced that all buses would leave at two o'clock. The pupils would be notified by radio whether there would be school next day.

Huddled in the vestibule, the youngsters from the island waited for their driver to bring the bus up to the door. Some of them were without raincoats. Luke silently blessed his mother for making him carry his slicker, for by now the rain was driving inland in sheets.

"Come on, kids," the driver shouted. "Pile aboard an' we'll try to navigate 'cross the bay."

By the time they reached the causeway there were big waves lashing the stone work. Two hours later and the tide would be high—a tide that might easily top the road-bed. The engine was missing on two cylinders, but the old bayman kept it chugging until at last they crossed the drawbridge over the channel and rolled down the other side onto the island. At his corner Luke got out and ran for the house through the buffeting wind. He found his father at home.

"Not much business at the store," he explained. "We got the boards over the windows and locked up about noon. This may not be a hurricane but it sure is a real rough northeaster."

Luke got into dry clothes and checked the barometer.

The red pointer had crossed the twenty-nine mark and was still falling. There was a good deal of static on the radio, but the progress of the storm was broadcast every few minutes. Greta, it appeared, had not veered out to sea or gone inland. She was rolling up the coast, still at a fast clip, her center now somewhere off the Delaware Capes.

By four o'clock the wind had shifted from east to northeast, along the rim of the counter-clockwise, low-pressure disturbance. Luckily there were no real hurricane winds forecast. The gale held steady at under sixty miles an hour.

In the early dusk Luke put on his bathing trunks and slipped out the back door, heading for the beach. The air was colder than he expected. With the stabbing rain chilling him to the bone, he fought his way to the top of the nearest dune. It was worth the battle, he thought, as he stared out at the angry sea. Huge breakers were smashing in, far above the ordinary high-tide line. Some of the smaller cottages close to the beach were taking a bad pounding, and a few would probably be washed off their foundations.

Suddenly he wondered uneasily what it was like on the bay side of the island. With the wind at his back he raced across the highway and down the road to the landing. He was just in time. The rickety little dock was gone and his sneakbox, pulled up on land, was right at the edge of the lapping tide. Frantically he took hold of the light boat and dragged it fifty feet farther up the sandy slope. Then he went back for the mast and boom and leeboards. Fortunately the sail was safe in the garage.

Back at the house the shivering boy toweled himself dry and took the scolding given him by his worried parents.

At supper, with the wind still howling outside, the talk was naturally about storms. Luke's father remembered other northeasters that had wrecked hundreds of houses and backed up tides into the bay until the water was a foot deep right over the main road.

"I don't look for this one to be that bad," he said, "but there'll be plenty of damage. When I came past the Yacht Club basin this morning, there were still two or three sailboats moored there. One had upset and the rest were rocking till it looked as if the masts would be whipped right out of 'em."

"Gosh!" Luke exclaimed. "You'd think anybody lucky enough to own a boat would care enough about it to get it pulled out in the fall. I know darn well I would!"

There was still some wind and rain when morning came, but the storm's center had moved on toward New England. As far as the Jersey coast was concerned, the danger was past. School was open and the bus ran as usual.

For the rest of that week every able-bodied man on the island was busy. Cottages had to be shored up and repaired. Roofs that had lost shingles were patched, docks rebuilt, and boats that had sunk or drifted from their moorings were salvaged. Luke picked up a few dollars over the weekend helping with these jobs.

When Monday came, he saw Johnny Grasso on the school bus.

"Hey," said the Italian boy, "you know that green sailboat o' Holliger's? She's gone—washed away in the storm. They'd left her tied to their dock in the basin. Thought they might be usin' her again, I guess. Anyhow, old man Holliger came down Saturday to see if there was any damage to his house. When he heard about the Comet, he just laughed. Said it was good riddance—he'd already ordered a new boat that would make everybody sit up an' take notice."

"What happened to the *Haulfast*?" Luke asked. "Did anybody see her go?"

"Not that I know of. Must have slipped her moorings an' been blown out in the channel. Sunk, I guess."

✿   ✿   ✿

39

November was always a month Luke enjoyed. It meant the beginning of duck-hunting season. Bunkie knew it, too, and on frosty mornings he would go down to the landing and look longingly across to the marshes on the other side of the bay. When Luke started repainting his decoys, the big black dog watched, quivering with excitement.

Like all Labradors, he was a one-man dog. The man who bred him and gave him his preliminary training had watched the young retriever's behavior the day Luke and his father had driven into the yard. The boy—he had been only fourteen then—had knelt beside the dog and put a hand on his wide black head. That did it. A moment later Bunkie had trotted off to his kennel and brought a battered old shoe to lay adoringly at Luke's feet.

"I reckon he's your dog," the owner had said with a wry grin. "He'll never be happy with anybody else. You'd better take him along right now, Mr. Cramer. We'll work out his price in trade at your store. I could get two hundred dollars for him easy from one o' the city sports, but you can have him for half that."

Seth Cramer never regretted the bargain. He knew that Luke would not only have a staunch comrade but would gain in patience and understanding as he continued the Labrador's training. Now he was a finished retriever, as good a gun dog as any in the county. He would even find upland birds such as quail or woodcock—not with the finished grace of a pointer or setter, but well enough for the purpose.

For weeks before the season opened, ducks were streaming south along the coastal flyway. Luke often rowed his sneakbox across the bay, without a gun, but with Bunkie as a passenger. He liked to watch the flights come in and make note of their favorite feeding grounds. There were black ducks and mallards and a few redheads. Canvasbacks were rare in the area.

The black dog sat perfectly still in the boat, but his ears reacted to every quack and his nose wrinkled in pleased anticipation. On the day when Luke brought the shotgun down for cleaning and oiling, the big retriever could hardly contain himself. He galloped to the shed and returned with a mallard decoy held gently in his mouth.

Luke chuckled as the wooden bird was laid at his feet. "Two more days, boy," he told Bunkie. "Two more days and we'll hit the marsh. Think you can wait that long?"

The two days passed slowly, and the weather, which had been fine for a week, turned cloudy and overcast. Friday there were spits of snow in the air and a skim of ice on the puddles. Saturday would be the big day.

Luke was up before four that morning. He tiptoed down and got his own breakfast. When he turned a flashlight on the outdoor thermometer, it stood at twenty-nine, but he had been on the marsh before and was prepared for the cold. Over a suit of heavy woolen underwear he wore a flannel shirt, two sweaters, and a canvas shooting coat. Two pairs of thick wool socks were under his waterproof high rubber shoes.

Outside in the dark he could hear Bunkie whining softly. He took his gun and a pocketful of shells, and when he opened the back door, the big dog fairly danced for joy.

Luke had to use the flashlight to get down to the landing, for it was still a good hour before dawn and there were no stars in the cloudy sky. He launched the sneakbox, settled Bunkie at his feet in the cockpit, and rowed across the quiet, mile-wide bay.

As he neared the sedgy bank on the other side, a sound of distant honking reached him through the earflaps of his cap. Very high and far away an arrow-flight of great gray Canada geese was winging south. The Labrador, of course, had heard them first. He lay quiet, but his black ears were standing out from his head and his teeth showed in a blissful grin.

Luke paddled through the shallow water into a tidal pond that looked like a good place for ducks. There he set out his decoys—two blacks, a bright-colored mallard drake, and a pair of grayish-brown mallard ducks. When they were floating naturally in a pattern that suited him, the boy poled his sneakbox back among the screening reeds and sat down to wait, the loaded gun across his knees.

Back of him he could hear the distant chug of car engines as hunters from the mainland came down to the marsh. There were duck blinds in plenty to the north of his position but none very close. After a while the car noises stopped. The gunners were waiting for daylight and the first stirring of the flocks.

A faint, distant quacking alerted Luke and made him forget the cold. Against the graying dawn sky he saw specks moving south. A gun blasted off to his left, then another and another. Crazy city folks, he thought. Firing at impossible ranges and too early to be legal. All they'd do would be to scare the ducks off.

Half an hour before sunrise, when the light was barely good enough for shooting, he saw half a dozen ducks veer over toward his decoys and brake with their wings. The low-voiced quacking told him they were talking it over, trying to decide whether the place was safe. He had no duck-call with which he could reassure them and the decoys were sitting too still to be all they seemed. With sudden decision the little flock picked up speed again and was gone before Luke could get a shot. Bunkie's amber eyes were sad and reproving.

"That's okay, boy," Luke told him in a low voice. "There'll be more."

He wished he could be as sure of it as he tried to sound. Ducks were flying all right, big flocks and small. But they didn't seem to be coming in to land. Another fifteen minutes passed and it would soon be sunrise—too late to move without being seen. Hastily the boy pulled in the decoys and paddled southward along a narrow tide creek. Just as he came around a bend, he saw black ducks feeding in the shallow water ahead.

He stood up in the boat and took the safety catch off the gun. It made only the slightest click, but in the next instant the ducks took off with a splash and a whirr of wings. It was a long shot—over fifty yards—but he leveled the gun and let go with both barrels. By luck he got a hit. One of the ducks turned a somersault in the air and dropped fluttering into the water.

Bunkie was up, both forefeet braced on the forward deck, waiting tense and quivering for his master's order. Luke gave it with a grin.

"Go fetch!" he said, and almost before the words were out of his mouth the retriever hit the water in a long leap. His thick black undercoat protected him from the icy cold and he swam like an arrow, straight for the floating duck. In less than two minutes he was back with the trophy, paddling alongside till Luke took it from his jaws.

"Good dog," said the boy. "Now go ashore and shake before you get back in the boat."

Bunkie understood and obeyed. When he had sprayed salt water all over the landscape, Luke paddled close to the bank and let him come back aboard.

They could hear the thin quacking of feeding ducks farther to the south. Instead of setting his decoys again, Luke decided to paddle on in the direction of the sound, hoping for another surprise shot. He chose a narrow creek that wound along inside the edge of the marsh and moved the sneakbox forward, careful to make no noise. Perhaps there would be ducks around the next bend.

But it wasn't ducks he found there. This time the surprise was all his own.

43

5

Beyond the bend the little tide creek ended in a muddy slough. On the right was the marsh. On the left a low sand bar, overgrown with reeds and salt grass, was all that separated the slough from the bay. And there, right in front of him, Luke saw the green-painted hull of a Comet, half buried in the mud.

He knew, even before he reached it, that the boat was Mert Holliger's *Haulfast*. It lay on its side, the broken mast in the water along with a tangle of wire that had been stays and standing rigging.

Trying to figure how the wreck got there, he remembered that the tide must have been well over the sand bar during the evening of the big storm. Probably the boat had capsized when she was torn from her moorings, and the gale from the east had drifted her right across the bay and over the submerged bar. After that she had lain stranded in the slough, her side sinking deeper into the muck with every tide.

Pulling her free now would be a hopeless task for one boy in a sneakbox. There was no way to tell how much her hull was damaged or whether she was worth salvaging at all.

Somehow the fun had gone out of duck-hunting for that

morning. Distant guns were still banging away to the north of him, but the only ducks he saw were flying high. He backed the little boat out of the slough and started rowing home.

After he had cleaned the duck and eaten a second breakfast, Luke got on his bicycle and rode down the island to Bruce Canning's office. He knew the real estate man had charge of the caretakers who looked after the bigger estates in the winter.

Canning was in and glad to see him. "Hi, sailor," he said. "I thought you'd be over on the marsh, first day of the season. Or did you shoot your limit already?"

"I got one," Luke told him. "But there's something else on my mind right now. You remember that green Comet of Holliger's?"

"Yes. I heard she was washed away in the northeaster. Nobody's been able to find her."

"Well," said Luke, "I found her—what there is left of her."

He described the slough and the appearance of the boat. "It might be possible to get her out," he said, "if Mr. Holliger were willing to pay for it. What do you think?"

Canning shook his head. "Mr. Holliger's a hard man to figure. But I may be talking to him on the phone today. I'll see what he has to say. Would you want to make an offer for the boat?"

Luke hesitated, desire struggling with common sense. "It's hard to tell whether the hull's still solid," he replied. "Probably hasn't been there long enough for worms to get into her, but the planking might be stove in, underneath, where you can't see it. I guess making any kind of an offer would be like buying a pig in a poke."

He thought about it as he rode home. If the hull was sound and could be brought ashore, he might have the start of the new Comet he wanted so much. And he knew somebody who would help him. Axel Gundersen, from up at Mizzen Inlet, was in his class at school. His father, Chris Gundersen, built bank skiffs for the colony of Norwegian fishermen at that end of the island. Axel, he was pretty sure, could borrow a power boat and give him a hand with towing the hull home.

That afternoon the telephone rang. Bruce Canning was on the line. "I talked to Mr. Holliger," he told Luke. "He didn't have much interest in salvaging the old boat. Says he's got a new one ordered for delivery in the spring and he was planning to get rid of this one anyhow. When I told him where it was and the condition it was in, he put a price on it that might make the job worth your while. He'll sell it for an even hundred dollars and throw in the sails. What do you say to that?"

Luke gulped a couple of times. He knew it was a gamble but he might never have another chance like this.

"I—I'll take it!" he blurted. "I can give you the money today."

"Hold on," Canning laughed. "There's no such rush as all that. Hadn't you better wait till you've had a look at the hull? If it's sound, you've really got a bargain. If it's busted up and in bad shape, you'd be wasting your money. Let me know some time the first part of the week."

With his head in a whirl, Luke called up Axel Gundersen. The young Norwegian was just in from a duck hunt and sounded sleepy, but he said he would come down early the next morning.

"Maybe I can get my dad interested," he added. "He knows plenty about boats."

Luke passed up church that Sunday. By eight o'clock he was down at the landing, watching the rising tide. If Axel timed it right, they might reach the Comet when the water was highest, and have an easier job pulling her free.

Half an hour later he saw the dory-like prow of a bank

47

skiff coming down the bay. There were two figures in the boat. Axel had persuaded his father to come with him.

Luke had met Chris Gundersen before. He was a big, weather-beaten, smiling man, his shock of blond hair now mostly gray. At his suggestion they tied the sneakbox on astern.

"Maybe this boat draws too much water to get in real close," he said. "We find out when we get there."

The skiff was broad-beamed and seaworthy, built for running through the rips on the inlet bar and fishing fifteen or twenty miles out. She had a rugged inboard engine that gave her about ten knots, even when loaded to the gunwales with fish.

Luke guided them to the tide creek that led into the slough and they chugged along it at low speed. The tide, as he had hoped, was nearing full flood. After a few minutes the skiff scraped a mud bank and Luke decided to lead the way in the sneakbox. He poled ahead, calling the depth of the water as it showed on his oar. There was still about four feet when he reached the bend at the entrance to the slough, and Chris Gundersen followed cautiously with the engine barely turning over.

"Okay," the older man called. "I can see the green boat from here. You an' Axel take this line over an' make it fast."

Axel joined Luke in the sneakbox, carrying a coil of stout three-quarter-inch manila rope. The high water seemed to have loosened the Comet a little. Kneeling on the foredeck of the sneakbox and heaving at the sailboat's side, Luke was able to lift it an inch or two.

Axel jumped into the water, his rubber boots sinking in the mud. With a struggle he got to the bow of the boat, which was nearer the bank. "Now!" he said. "Both together!"

There was a sucking sound as the buried side came out

of the muck. Then Axel kicked his feet free and scrambled back into the sneakbox. Luke meanwhile was tying an end of the line firmly to a cleat on the sailboat's stern. They poled across to the skiff, fifty feet away, and tossed the other end of the rope aboard. A moment later they were backing slowly out of the creek with the green hull towing obediently after them.

At the mouth of the little waterway there was a deep-washed channel with a firm bank beside it. The elder Gundersen brought the skiff close to the bank, holding on by a boat hook, and stopped the engine.

"No mud here," he said. "An' there's enough water to turn her over if you don't mind gettin' wet. We better see how her bottom an' port side look before we tow her home."

While Axel hauled in on the tow rope, Luke went over the side into four feet of water. It was cold, but there was no time to think about that. First he jerked the stump of the broken mast out of its step. The tangled wire rigging would have to wait for work on shore. The boom was still attached to the base of the mast and seemed to be un-damaged. He pushed the spars and wire over to Axel's waiting hands and turned his attention to the hull.

Because of the load of mud that had settled in the port side, he found it impossible to tip the boat from that di-rection. Working his way around to the deep side, where he stood nearly up to his neck in water, he got his hands under the edge of the centerboard well and heaved with all his might.

Loggily the muck-filled hull turned bottom up. Luke rubbed with his hands at the mud, scraping some of it off.

"She's solid!" he called through chattering teeth. "No breaks in her planking!"

"All right," Chris Gundersen told him with a grin, "get back aboard before you freeze to death."

They hauled the chilled boy in over the gunwale and went across the bay at good speed despite the pull of the double tow.

"We'll take care o' gettin' out the sneakbox an' the sailboat," Axel told Luke. "You run quick up home an' change."

Luke just about made it to the house, tired and shaking with the cold. He stripped off his soggy clothes and got into a hot shower. Two or three minutes of that delightful warmth made him feel a lot better, and he rubbed himself down, put on dry clothes, and hurried back to the landing.

The Gundersens had done wonders in the short time he had been absent. Using the bailing bucket from the skiff, they had washed all the mud off the outside of the *Haulfast* and were busy getting the caked, sticky marsh muck out of her hold.

"You'll need a scrub brush an' a lot of elbow grease to get her real clean," said Axel. "But Dad says she's sound as a dollar. No worms an' no dry rot. You got yourself a pretty good boat."

Chris Gundersen was straightening out the two parts of the broken mast. He took a folding carpenter's rule from his pocket and measured the over-all length.

"I can get you a new stick for her," he said. "I've got a piece o' seasoned spruce that's long enough, an' you an' Axel can taper it down with a drawshave. Some o' this riggin's been too much snarled an' twisted to be any good, but the hardware seems to be pretty fair. Looks like you'll have plenty to do this winter, puttin' her in shape."

"Gosh!" said Luke. "I don't know how to thank you folks. I'd like to pay for the mast, Mr. Gundersen, if you'll tell me how much."

The older man chuckled. "I've had that piece for years," he said. "Probably got it for nothin'. When you're ready, you come up to my boat shop an' use the tools, any time."

They said good-by, and Luke spent the rest of the day scrubbing the hull. It was hard work, but he didn't mind. Every scrap of mud that came off brought him nearer to his dream.

That evening he counted up his cash. He had a hundred and six dollars and some odd change. He put the hundred in an envelope and pedaled down the island to Bruce Canning's home.

"Here's the money," he told the real estate man. "I thought I'd better bring it right now before I spend any of it."

"So you've decided the boat's worth buying," said Canning. "Have you had a good look—to make sure she's sound?"

Luke explained that the hull was already at his landing and reasonably clear of mud. "Near as I can tell," he said, "all she needs is a new mast and rigging. I'll sand her and paint her, too, of course. Do you think Mr. Holliger'll stick to his bargain?"

Canning nodded. "No question about that," he assured the boy. "I'll draw up a transfer of ownership for him to sign and get the sails and the certificate of measurement for you whenever you want them. But I guess there's no hurry about that. Later on, of course, you'll have to register the boat with the Comet Class Yacht Racing Association in your name."

Luke drew a deep breath. "Reckon I've got a lot to work and save for now," he said with a grin. "But I'll make it somehow. I've got plenty to thank you for, skipper. And I hope you won't mind if I don't crew for you next summer."

"Not a bit," Canning told him. "I'll be proud to have a pupil of mine sailing his own boat—but I won't promise not to beat the daylights out of you when we're in the same race!"

Before he went to bed that night, Luke wrote a long

letter to Marilyn March. There was a lot to tell. He described the storm and his discovery of the wrecked *Haulfast*.

"I've bought her," he continued proudly, "and I'm going to try to fix her up. Next time you see her she'll be painted a different color and have a new name. You said something once about wishing you could sail with me, and I hope you still want to. If I can get the boat in shape, we'll both learn a lot."

6

Luke worked like a beaver in those early days of December. As soon as he had finished washing out the Comet, he borrowed a light trailer and brought the hull up to the house. They had a two-car garage, half of which was full of accumulated junk. One of his first jobs was to clear it out and give himself a clean, sheltered place to work. There was no heat in the garage, but at least he was out of the wind and the weather, and the precious boat was safe.

Each night after school he would rush out as soon as he had changed his clothes and work till suppertime, then put in another hour after he had eaten. He never had time for television, and it is quite possible his homework suffered.

When the thorough cleaning of the woodwork was finished, he took off every bit of hardware—the cleats, chocks, pulleys, bow ring and traveler, the big bronze centerboard, and even the rudder eyes. Next he started to work with coarse sandpaper, taking off the paint down to the bare wood.

It was an almost endless task. He was still at it Saturday morning, and Bunkie watched him from the doorway, his eyes reproachful. What his young master was doing must have seemed silly enough, right in the middle of duck-hunting time.

Once Luke saw the big dog start up, trembling, and look off to the west. Going to the door the boy shaded his eyes and made out a distant smudge in the sky—a big flock of ducks. The Labrador's keen ears had caught their quacking, too faint for Luke to hear.

"Doggone it, boy," Luke said, laughing, "you've convinced me. I've got all winter to fix up the boat. We'll go over there and have a try."

They were too late that morning, for the sun was already high. But twice during the following week Luke rose before five o'clock and reached the marsh in time for the dawn flights. They got half a dozen ducks, all told.

On Friday night the boy heard a clear, high honking that meant the winter brant were coming in. There were fewer of the little black geese than in earlier times and there had been a ban on shooting them. Now the eel grass on which they fed was coming back, and flocks of brant were more numerous. The game laws now allowed them to be hunted.

Luke was up very early the next morning. The wind was still, but the temperature hung close to the freezing mark as he rowed out across the bay in the darkness. Bunkie sat huddled with him in the cockpit.

Brant, the boy knew from experience, had their own kind of caution. It was no use looking for them in the tidal channels and pools of the marsh. They wouldn't fly across land—not even across a grassy bar. The only chance for a shot was when they came in to feed in shoal water along the edge of the bay itself.

Luke chose an inlet that ran behind a narrow, reed-covered island, and pulled the sneakbox up on the bank where it would be out of sight when daylight came. Then, carrying the gun and followed by the dog, he crossed to the bay shore. At the point where he came out, he knew there was a sheltered cove where shallows and a weedy bottom might offer feed.

He picked a spot four or five feet from the bank. High reeds would screen him on either side, but he had a fair view of the cove. He spread a poncho over the mud for a seat and crouched there, pulling Bunkie close so that they could keep each other warm.

It was a long, cold wait. He was beginning to think the sun would never rise when at last the sky paled and a light breeze sprang up from the northeast. The big Labrador beside him shivered a little with anticipation and Luke saw his ears lift.

"What is it, boy?" he whispered. "You hear something?"

There was no honking, but suddenly he heard the flap of wings borne toward them on the breeze. Then he saw a flock of eight or ten big birds scudding low over the water. As if at some silent signal they wheeled into the cove and completed the hundred-and-eighty-degree turn to land into the wind.

It was still too dark for a good shot. Luke sat motionless, hardly breathing, and waited. Apparently the brant had no idea he was there, for first one, then another, tipped its tail high and put its beak down into the weeds at the bottom. Gradually more light came into the sky. When he could distinguish the black breasts from the lighter-colored under feathers, the boy slipped off his mitten, removed the safety catch, and raised the gun, all in one quick motion.

At the clicking sound every goose in the flock started its take-off. Luke fired one barrel, saw a brant tumble, and held his other shot.

"Go fetch, Bunkie!" he commanded. The dog had been waiting for the word. Quickly he brought the dead goose ashore, laid it proudly at Luke's feet, and went off into the reeds to shake himself.

"A brant's not much to brag about for eating," said the

boy with a grin. "I hope we're not short o' turkey because I'd hate to have this fellow for Christmas dinner. Now let's go home an' get warm."

*　　*　　*

Christmas vacation would give Luke more time to work on the boat. He had finished the big job of sanding and checked over the hardware and rigging. Fortunately for him, his father's store carried just about everything he would need. But even at wholesale prices, the replacements and the paint would come to fifty dollars at least. He just had to get out and earn some more money.

Again it was Bruce Canning who came to the rescue. There was a good deal of inside painting being done in hundreds of rental cottages, and some of the small contractors Canning employed were shorthanded. Armed with a note from the real estate man, Luke got a job as painter's helper at a dollar and a quarter an hour, and was given four days' work that week. When he was paid off, he had forty dollars in his pocket—enough to go ahead with the boat.

Three days before Christmas he got a call from Axel Gundersen.

"How about coming up here tomorrow morning?" his friend suggested. "We can have Dad's shop to ourselves, an' I've got that spar laid out, ready to work on. Do you know the right measurements for a Comet mast?"

"No, but I'll get 'em tonight. And I'll be on hand bright an' early. Thanks, Axel. See you tomorrow."

As Luke expected, Bruce Canning had a copy of the Comet Class Handbook. He went down that evening and made a careful copy of the mast dimensions. The height, he found, must be twenty feet, four inches above the deck line. The mast could be rectangular, circular, or oval in cross-section, and either solid or box construction. The

Sally C had a rectangular mast, but he knew that most of the Comets in the fleet used round ones.

The fore-and-aft thickness of the mast must be two and seven-eighths inches at a point six inches above the deck, tapering to one and three-eighths at the top. The 'thwart-ship thickness tapered from one and seven-eighths up to one and three-eighths inches. And the spreaders could be located anywhere from halfway up the mast to a foot or two higher.

It was nearly ten miles up the island to the inlet. Luke got his father to lend him the car and reached the little Gundersen boat yard by nine o'clock. Axel had the spruce stick laid out on a pair of carpenter's horses. It was beautiful wood, straight-grained and clear, without a sign of a knot.

"I sharpened up a couple o' drawshaves," said Axel. "Let's get those dimensions pinned to the wall, so we both know we aren't takin' off too much."

Luke had carefully measured the step, and knew the foot of the spar must be squared to fit it. With a steel tape they measured the length of the timber. Allowing eighteen inches for the portion below the deck line, they sawed it off with a total length of twenty-one feet, ten inches. Then they set to work to taper the mast down and round it off.

They took turns, one peeling off the long, curly shavings, the other measuring with calipers. When it was down to a quarter inch above dimensions, they used a plane, then switched to sandpaper. Occasionally Luke got down on his knees and sighted along the clean, yellow wood.

"Gosh!" he said. "It looks so good now, I'm scared to touch it. Sure would hate to make a mistake."

At four that afternoon Chris Gundersen came out to examine their handiwork. He, too, sighted along the mast, turning it over and over. He checked the required meas-

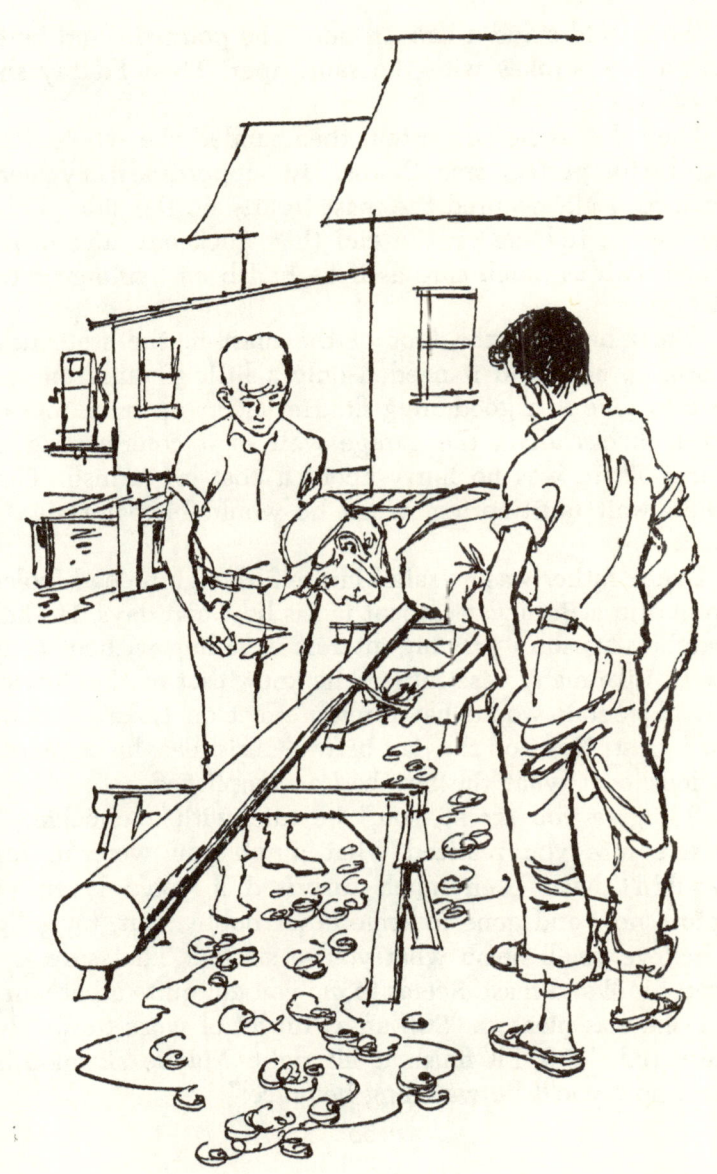

urements and applied the calipers at various points along it.

"She could stand a hair off here," he pointed, "and here. Just a few strokes with the sandpaper. Then I'd say she would do."

They did as he suggested, then sanded the whole spar lightly for perfect smoothness. By suppertime they were finished. Luke secured the mast tightly on the side of the car, tied a red rag on the end that stuck out, and drove home with as much care as if he had been hauling crates of eggs.

When he tried the foot of the mast in the step, next morning, he found it needed only a little planing on one side to give it a good snug fit. He laid it up on a row of level chocks along the garage wall so it couldn't sag or warp. There was no hurry about a coat of varnish. That could wait until spring, when he would be painting the boat.

Luke's father was no sailor himself, though he had fooled around in a Barnegat catboat in his boyhood days. He had watched his son's growing interest in sailing without comment. Like many wise fathers, he knew that neither advice nor objections would have much effect on Luke's passion for a boat. Now, on the day before Christmas, he came out to look over what the boy had accomplished.

"I'll give you credit, son," he said with a chuckle. "I wasn't sure you realized what a job you were in for. Wouldn't have been much surprised if you'd given up before now and gone to some other hobby. But, by golly, I believe you'll finish what you've started. That sure is a pretty hull and mast. Seems to me you got quite a bargain."

Luke was pleased. "Still an awful lot of work to do," he answered. "But I'll finish it all right. Maybe six months from now you'll be watching her race!"

"What do you plan to name her?" Seth Cramer asked. "I see you've scraped off the old name."

The boy hesitated, reddening a little. "Haven't made up my mind yet," he said, "but I'll think up a good name."

As a matter of fact he had debated calling the boat the *Marilyn*, but decided it would be taking a good deal for granted. He had only known the girl a few hours in all, and he'd look pretty silly if she went somewhere else next summer. Even worse if she continued to go around with the Holliger crowd. Probably he would wind up with some ordinary name, like *Seabird* or *Swordfish*.

That evening—Christmas Eve—the parcel-post truck delivered a package addressed to Luke. It was small, but it came from Marilyn and was marked "Do not open until Christmas." He put it with the pile of other presents under the tree, wishing his family opened gifts on Christmas Eve, as some other households did. After shaking the little package he knew it contained something light and soft. There was nothing in it that rattled.

They went to church and sang carols that night, then went to bed. Luke thought he had outgrown his childish excitement about Christmas, but he found himself eager to get to sleep so that morning would come sooner.

The early sun that woke him seemed brighter than usual. When he went to the window, he discovered why. It had snowed in the night—a light, fluffy two inches of snow that lay softly on the shrubbery and fences. It would be gone by noon, like most South Jersey snowfalls, but it made a lovely setting for Christmas morning.

Luke went down the hall hammering on doors and yelling "Merry Christmas." Then he dressed in a hurry and reached the kitchen just as his mother finished squeezing the orange juice. She had beaten him downstairs after all. They were soon joined by Joan and her father and ate their breakfast to the sound of holiday music on the radio.

"Now!" said Luke. "Let's open presents!"

"Not yet," Mrs. Cramer told him firmly. "You know the rule. You and Joanie do the dishes first."

At last the final plate was dried and put away. They trooped into the living room and gathered around the tree. Mrs. Cramer settled herself in an armchair with a pad and pencil.

"All right," she said. "Be sure to read the cards and tell me who sent each one, so I can keep a list. We want to thank all the people who remembered us."

They took turns opening their gifts. Not wanting to seem too anxious, Luke saved the little package till last, but he kept his eye on it. Among the presents he got were sport shirts and neckties from his mother, a box of shotgun shells from his Uncle Harry, a check for ten dollars from Aunt Bess, and several books—one of them called *Winning Sailboat Races*. That was from his sister, who had pretended to be so scornful of his sailing ambitions. Before she could duck he kissed her.

His next present was a plain envelope with his name in his father's handwriting. He opened it and gasped. It was a junior membership in the Man-o'-War Yacht Club. That had been one of his worries, for he knew it was expensive and he wouldn't be able to race without it.

"Gosh, Dad," he choked. "Thanks a heap! I guess you really are with me in this Comet business."

They were nearly finished with the presents now, and the gaudy wrapping paper lay in heaps around them. There was only one gift left for Luke.

"Come on," said Joan impishly. "Quit stalling—you've got to open it some time." She must have peeked at the sender's name.

He fumbled with the brown paper and string. Inside was another package in pretty Christmas wrapping, and inside that a small cardboard box. When he opened it, he found a bit of red silk and a note.

"Dear Luke," said the note. "In case you don't recognize this, it's a wind-sock for your new boat. I made it myself, so the stitches aren't as even as I'd like. It's from an old red silk party dress of mine. Good sailing and a fair wind!"

Carefully he unfolded the twelve-inch cone of silk. To his eye at least it was beautiful. There was a wide hem at the open end, which he could thread with a circle of fine wire and fasten to a spike in the masthead. Then he would have a really serviceable wind direction finder—a lot better looking than the brant's wing feather he had planned to use.

He wrote Marilyn that night, enclosed a snapshot of the boat's hull, taken the day he had finished taking off the paint, and apologized for not having sent her a Christmas gift. "All my cash is tied up in the Comet," he explained, "but if she turns out all right, I hope I can make it up to you next summer with a lot of sailing."

7

Before the winter holidays ended, Luke made a list of all the marine hardware he would need. Reading the Comet Class Yacht Racing Rules, he discovered there were other necessities to be bought as well. Every boat entered in a race had to carry an anchor and anchor rope and two kapok cushion life preservers. Figuring up his assets once more, and adding the ten dollars from Aunt Bess, he decided he could just about do it—maybe with a little work on the side if he could find a job.

Back at school, Johnny Grasso talked to him at lunch one day.

"Know what I heard?" said the shoemaker's son. "Bill Reach, at the boat yard, says old man Holliger's ordered a fiberglas hull for Mert's new Comet. You know—they've tried out one or two of 'em, but the Rules Committee hasn't said yet whether they're okay to race. I bet Holliger's pullin' plenty o' strings to get 'em accepted!"

"Hmm," said Luke thoughtfully. "So that's the secret weapon he said he'd give his son. It'll sure save a lot o' painting an' rubbing to keep the finish slick. But I still think the way a boat's handled in a race is what really counts."

Lying in bed that night, he wondered if there was any way to make fiberglas green. There had better be, he told himself with a grin. Any boat young Mert Holliger owned would have to be the Haulfast Truck Lines color. Personally he thought white, common as it was, made a Comet hull prettier than anything else. In the big fleet that sailed in the bay there were red boats, black ones, grays and tans, blues and yellows. But most of the consistent winners seemed to be painted white.

When Saturday came, he set the hull up on chocks and poured about six inches of water in with the hose. Then he lay underneath and waited to see where she leaked, if at all. A few drops oozed out at the point where the stem and bottom joined. The dripping stopped as soon as the wood began to swell, but he decided it could stand a bit of caulking and some white lead. One other wet spot appeared at a corner of the transom, where it met the side planking, and again he marked the place for caulking.

When he had dumped out the water and the overturned boat was dry once more, he got out a small reel of cotton wicking. Two or three strands were all he needed, and he worked them carefully into the seam with the edge of a putty knife. After they were tight, he covered the spots with white lead and smoothed it down.

Luke knew his father could give him good advice on paint, for he sold a lot of it to boatmen. They talked it over that evening.

"You plan to keep her moored in the water?" Seth Cramer asked.

"No," Luke told him. "I've seen too many boats that dragged their moorings on a high tide, and banged into docks and other boats. I'd like to build a little trailer and haul her out each time I use her."

His father nodded. "Then you don't need copper or bronze bottom paint. All they're for is keeping off barnacles and weed. I'd use the same paint all over her—at least five or six coats, sanded down each time. That's the only way to get a good racing finish, they tell me. And while you're at it, use good paint. You'll find it pays—covers better and lasts better."

There was no hurry about starting the painting. Luke knew he should wait till there was no danger of freezing weather. But he was concerned about the trailer he had mentioned to his father. He talked to Axel Gundersen about it at school. Together they went to an automobile junkyard on the outskirts of Marshtown during the noon hour. The owner had little business in the off season, and when he heard what they were after, he took a real interest.

"Back here somewhere," he said, leading the way to the rear of the lot, "seems to me I've got an old pair o' Ford wheels. Off an early Model A they are—maybe thirty years old."

It took a few minutes to find them, and when they were finally located, they looked pretty bad. Luke saw the rust on the rims and axle and the half-disintegrated tires and his heart sank.

"Think we could do anything with junk like that?" he asked his friend.

"Yep," said Axel. "I bet you'll be surprised. Tires are no good, o'course." He turned to the dealer. "Got a pair of old casings that'll fit those rims—something good enough for a light trailer?"

The man nodded. "I'll tell you," he said. "I'd forgot how lousy those wheels were. Ought to get 'em off the lot anyhow. I'll give 'em to you an' just charge for the tires. Three dollars apiece including tubes that'll hold air."

It sounded cheap enough. "Okay," said Luke. "If you'll keep 'em here for me, I'll bring the car over an' pick 'em up this weekend."

On Saturday he put a tow rope in the Buick, along with a piece of scantling, and drove over to Marshtown. To his

surprise the wheels were standing out in front, already fitted with fairly good tires. The junk dealer had even rubbed off much of the rust on the wheels and axle with crankcase oil.

"Didn't have anything else to do," he explained, "so I thought I'd make 'em look a little better."

He helped Luke tie the scantling firmly to the middle of the axle and hitch the tow rope to the front end.

"You'll have to get a license an' a taillight for that when it's finished," he said, "but I reckon no cops'll stop you before you get it home. Goin' to use it for a boat trailer?"

Luke told him about the Comet and paid him the six dollars. Then, driving slowly to avoid any whipping, he made his way back across the causeway to the island. The wheels bumped along behind, squeaking a bit but towing without trouble.

He had seen a good many boat trailers at the Yacht Club and had a fair idea how one should be built. One thing he knew he would need was a pair of leaf springs. He'd have to go back to the junkyard for those, but they shouldn't cost much. He had enough lumber around to build a frame eight or ten feet long. The spring shackles could be bolted to the under side of the frame, and attached to the two ends of the axle at the thick part of the spring. Then he could saw out a couple of two-by-sixes to make cradles that would fit the boat bottom, and mount them on top of the frame. Padded with an old piece of carpet, they would carry the hull safely.

First of all he had to take off the wheels and see if the bearings were any good. He did it that afternoon and found them badly worn. However, they would have only light work to do so he packed them with heavy grease and put the wheels back on. The squeak, at least, was gone.

While he was at work, Axel Gundersen came down to see how things were going. Together they measured, sawed, and nailed a solid frame of three-by-fours. It had cross braces a foot from each end, which would serve not only to strengthen the frame but to hold the cradles. From what would be the forward end they extended a towing tongue, angle-braced to keep it firm.

Axel laughed. "This thing's goin' to work, all right," he said, "but it'll weigh twice as much as the boat!"

"Just about," Luke agreed. "But for what I want to do with it, that won't matter."

When they went into the house for a coke they found it was only three-thirty. Axel had come in his old jaloppy. He offered to drive over to Marshtown to hunt for springs, and Luke got a little money and went with him.

The man at the auto graveyard was about to close for the day, but when they told him their problem he took them to a rack at the back of the shop.

"Transverse springs from old Fords," he said. "I got a million of 'em. Not much demand any more. I'll let you have 'em for a buck apiece. That's pretty near the price o' scrap iron."

Pleased with his bargain, Luke took the springs home, cleaned them up and put them to soak in oil to get the rust and squeaks out of them. That was as far as they got that weekend, but before January ended the boys had finished the trailer. As Axel had forecast, it was heavy and clumsy, but it towed squarely and did no yawing. If Luke wanted to use it for trips to races at other clubs, he would have to get a vehicle license for it and rig up some kind of taillight. But for moving the boat around near home, he would hardly need them.

His next project was the standing rigging. He had already whittled out a pair of spreaders and figured where they should be mounted on the mast. Now he went down to the big covered shed at the boat yard, where a lot of the local Comets were stored. Bill Reach, who ran the place in the winter, had heard about his purchase of the old *Haulfast.*

"Good boat," he commented. "Young Holliger never got the most out of her, the way I see it. She was Riverton-built, an' they're tops. How's her spars an' rigging?"

Luke told him about the homemade mast. "It's the rigging I wanted to talk to you about," he said. "Stainless steel wire's the best, isn't it? That's what she had before, but it got pretty well fouled up."

The boatman nodded. "Bring it down here," he said. "Let me take a look—see if any of it's worth salvaging."

The boy went home and loaded the upper part of the old mast and the snarl of wire into the Buick trunk. When he returned, Reach started methodically to untangle it, clucking in dismay.

"Durn fools!" he grumbled. "Wouldn't have been any trouble for Mr. Holliger to call up an' tell me to haul her out. I thought o' callin' him, but by the time the storm hit we were too busy on other folks' boats."

He straightened out one piece of wire and examined it. "Headstay," he said. "No bad kinks in this one, anyhow."

When he finished, he told Luke that about half the standing rigging would do. "The lower shrouds are in fair shape," he said. "Upper shrouds I wouldn't trust, the way they're messed up."

Luke was relieved. He might get by on the money he had, after all. On Reach's recommendation he went to his father's store and bought several gallons of top quality paint, one for the primer coat, the rest for a high gloss enamel finish. There were some good brushes in the garage, but before he used them he soaked them overnight in turpentine to get them thoroughly clean.

He didn't rush the painting, but worked only when the weather was mild. Each coat he put on was allowed to

70

dry for two days. Then he rubbed it down with fine, wet sandpaper. It was early March before he applied the last coat of enamel. That was on one of the warm, sunny days that sometimes come to the coast at the beginning of spring. He had moved the hull outside where it rested on the trestles, gleaming white in the sun.

Johnny Grasso rode into the yard on his bike and stood admiring the boat.

"Golly, man!" he said. "You sure can see your face in that finish. Can I touch it?"

"Not on your life!" Luke told him. "That's got hours to dry yet."

"I bet she'll slide through the water," said Johnny. "I s'pose you got a name for her?"

Luke nodded. "I'm going to call her the *Tern*."

The Italian boy gaped at him. "Turn? What kind o' turn? Like 'U-turn' or 'No left turn'?"

"No, you dope—*Tern*—the bird that flies along over the surf. It's nearly all white, with a little black cap and an orange bill."

"Oh, those," said Johnny doubtfully. "I always thought they were just small gulls. I'll admit they're pretty, though. I was figurin' maybe you'd follow Mert Holliger's lead an' call her somethin' like 'Cramer's Highgrade Hardware.'"

Luke smiled but he didn't think his friend was particularly funny. He had been rather proud of the name when he finally decided on it. To him the tern was the most graceful of all seabirds. Besides, it was a short name—only four letters. He wasn't much of an artist, but he thought he could make a fairly good job of painting such a short word.

For the brightwork inside the hull, and for the mast, boom, and tiller, Luke used spar varnish. Again he gave it two good coats, sanding down the first one after it was

71

dry. Proudly he looked at the number cut into the starboard side of the centerboard well—3095—in neatly carved figures over two inches tall.

It was *his* number now. Every Comet got a registration number when she was built, and it stayed with her for life, no matter how many times she might be sold.

Before Easter the *Tern* was as far along as paint and varnish would take her. Luke had saved all the undamaged hardware and tackle that had been on the boat originally. He burnished it up now, and put each cleat, chock, and eye-bolt on where it belonged. He also bought two pairs of patented grip clamps that would hold a sheet or halliard firmly as long as there was a pull on it, and release the line in an instant when the helmsman hauled the opposite way.

For the upper shrouds he purchased new stainless steel aircraft wire of the same thickness as the old, and fitted it to the turnbuckles. With Axel Gundersen's help he stepped the mast and rerigged the whole boat during one busy weekend. The running rigging was new manila line. He couldn't afford one of the synthetic fibers, and he knew manila would wear well and not stretch too much.

When everything was on her except the sails, and every line taut and shipshape, Luke painted her name on the transom. He used low, square block letters, traced from newspaper advertisements, and he labored hard over the delicate job. Last of all, he put the little red wind-sock at the truck. Then he brought the camera from the house, and in the bright April sunshine he took two or three color pictures. From the best one he had a print made and sent it to Marilyn March.

8

The Regional Measurer of the Comet Class Yacht Racing Association was a Dr. Lloyd Seeley. He was a retired mathematics professor, living now in Foremast Harbor. The spry, gray little man had done some sailboat racing in his younger days and still took a keen interest in the Comet fleets along the coast.

When Luke telephoned him and explained how he had bought and repaired the Holliger boat, Dr. Seeley agreed at once to come up to the house. First he checked the original certificate of measurement that had come with the transfer papers. Then with a steel tape he went over every inch of the *Tern*. At his request, Luke released the standing rigging and unstepped the mast. The doctor measured it twice.

"You're a quarter of an inch over the standard height," he said. "But the rules allow a half-inch of leeway, so it passes as satisfactory. You made this mast yourself?"

Luke told him how Chris Gundersen had donated the spruce stick and let the boys use his shop.

"You're lucky," the professor remarked. "It's a beauty—good as any professional job. Now let's have a look at the sails."

Luke had brought them from Bruce Canning's house, along with the papers, the week before. He chose a level

73

spot on the lawn and spread them out so that they could be measured.

"This is just a formality," Dr. Seeley explained. "They passed when the boat was first registered. That's a nice suit of sails, and they seem to have been well cared for. It's a pity Holliger didn't use the same care with the hull and mast. But after the work you've done on her I'd say this Comet is in as good shape as she ever was. I'll send the measurements to headquarters and you'll be getting your new certificate in a few days."

Luke paid him the measurer's fee and they shook hands.

"Good luck!" the little professor said. "I expect I'll be watching you race from the Judges' Deck next summer."

Eager as he was to get the boat in the water, Luke decided to wait for the settled weather that would come later in the spring. There was a good deal of rain in April and he knew frequent wettings wouldn't be good for the sails.

Meanwhile he played as first-string catcher on the high school baseball team, and with daily practice and week-end games he had few chances to do any sailing.

He liked to play ball. Axel Gundersen was the team's star pitcher and they had worked together for two seasons. Luke knew how to handle the big fellow's fast ball and slider, and when Axel showed signs of wildness, he knew how to steady him down.

They had no rivals near by, so most of their games were played with schools thirty or forty miles away. Traveling by bus, they met one team after another up and down the coast and won their fair share of victories, though they didn't get into the regional play-offs. By the middle of May the schedule was completed.

"Axel," said Luke, as they rode home from their final Friday afternoon game, "how'd you like to do some sailing tomorrow?"

The tall pitcher grinned. "You know me," he said. "Any time. You aimin' to try out the *Tern*?"

"That's right," Luke nodded. "I've got a heap to learn before Memorial Day, when the races start. Looks like a fair day and a strong breeze tomorrow, and I need a good heavy crew man to keep her right side up."

"I'm your boy," Axel answered. "You just call the signals, like you do behind the plate. Want to get an early start?"

"Well, let's plan on ten o'clock. I'll be looking for you then."

Luke had bent the sails on when the Norwegian boy arrived. He had tried them before and they seemed to fit well. Now he hauled them down and stowed them loosely in the cockpit, with the sloop still on the trailer. They had no trouble wheeling her down to the landing, where a ramp of planks led directly into the bay. At the basin behind the Yacht Club there was a new electric hoist that picked up a Comet and lowered her neatly into the water. For the present, however, Luke was quite content to use the trailer and ramp.

They made the *Tern* fast to the dock while they pulled the trailer out. Then both got down into the boat and hoisted sail. Finally Luke fitted the rudder on the stern and took the five-foot tiller, with its folded extension rod, in his left hand. There are no seats in a Comet. The helmsman and crew both sit on the deck to windward, with their feet in the cockpit.

"Ready to cast off," Luke commanded, and Axel obeyed with a grin and a smart "Aye, aye, Skipper." The westerly breeze filled the sails from starboard, the centerboard was dropped, and the sloop heeled neatly over on a southwestward tack.

"Boy!" Axel murmured. "This is the life. Look at the sweet way that mainsail draws!"

Luke, more critical, eyed the leech and adjusted the

outhaul a trifle. "There," he said, "that's better. Foots along nicely, doesn't she?"

"Sure does. Look—there's a couple of other boats out there. Want to give 'em a race?"

Luke shook his head. "All I want today is to get the feel of her—see how she handles, tacking, reaching, and running free. We'll practice coming about in a minute or two. This wind is light now, but I have a hunch it's going to freshen up before noon."

Luke had always marveled at the craftsmanship that went into a good suit of sails. These bore the proud label of experts in New York, and were made of stout nylon, lighter and stronger than cotton canvas. Just above the boom, about midway forward in the mainsail, there was a foot-square "window" of clear plastic that allowed him to see through to leeward.

But what he admired most was the roach tailored into the sail—the subtle curve like that of an airplane wing. It created a vacuum on the outer side of the curve, and gave the boat forward pull just as the wing gives lift to a plane.

Now he was pointing as high as he could and he noticed a flutter in the luff of the mainsail. The Comet slowed perceptibly.

"Jib sheet's trimmed too tight," Axel suggested. "She's back-winding the mainsail."

Luke leaned forward to slack the sheet an inch or two and the trouble disappeared like magic. "Thanks," he said. "I should have known that. I've seen Bruce Canning do it a dozen times. Okay—ready to come about."

He put the helm down and the bow swung into the wind. They ducked under the boom and squared away on the port tack. Luke was reveling in the feeling of quick response he got from the boat. He held the tiller, not hard in his fist, but lightly, letting the sloop talk to him through

76

his fingers. That way he seemed able to anticipate the *Tern*'s movements—know just when she needed a bit more helm or a touch on the sheet. It made him almost a part of her swiftness and grace. He had never done any riding but he thought this must be how a horseman felt about a good horse.

They went nearly to the other side of the bay on the port tack, then fell away on a northward reach as the breeze freshened. The boat heeled far to leeward and they both perched high on the weather side, hooking their feet in the hiking straps. Below, along the sleek side and bottom of the sloop, the waves slapped and gurgled.

"Gee!" exclaimed Axel. "Who wants a motorboat when he can have this? I bet we're doin' ten miles an hour!"

They slanted back to the eastward before the wind, experimented with a jibe or two, then sailed down the bay on another reach. Axel was a good sailor, and Luke invited him to take the helm on the return trip. The Norwegian boy was more than delighted.

"You've got yourself a real winner," he said, when they tied up at the dock. "I've been in a couple of other good Comets, but never one as slick as this."

After that Luke left the boat on the trailer down by the landing. He had her out weekends and evenings practically every day that the weather was fair. Sometimes he took Johnny Grasso, sometimes Axel. Occasionally, in a light breeze, he sailed with only the dog, Bunkie, for company. For proper handling, any sailboat with a jib really needs a two-man crew, but Luke found he could manage the simpler maneuvers fairly well by himself.

Once, late in May, he nearly got in trouble. He was two miles from home, down the bay beyond the Yacht Club one afternoon. Glancing back to the northward, he saw a black cloud beginning to pile up. The breeze was still very light, and what there was came from the south.

As quickly as he could the boy pulled the boat around to run before the wind for home. He knew it wouldn't be long till there was a shift, but the suddenness of it caught him unprepared. A fast-moving line of dark water appeared right ahead, and before he could do anything about it the squall hit from the north. It took the Comet all aback. Her sails slatted and her boom swung wildly inboard, barely missing Luke's head.

He jerked the tiller toward him, hauled in the main sheet with frantic haste, and hooked his feet in the hiking strap as the boat heeled over to starboard. Luckily the new stays held in spite of the sudden strain. Bunkie had moved instinctively when the gust came, and he clung as far out to windward as he could get, his hind feet braced against the centerboard well. Luke leaned out with him, gritting his teeth and hanging on, praying silently that they wouldn't go over.

Somehow they made it. The fury of the squall grew less and the *Tern* scudded on. There came a momentary lull and another shift of wind. This time the gusts blew from a more westerly direction, though the thundercloud was still north of them. Luke saw lightning flashing and heard the ominous rumble that followed. He watched the water more carefully and was ready when the wind, still shifting, came screaming up from the southwest. He had never had time to trim the jib, and the smaller sail had been flapping while the sloop tacked. Now, as he slacked the main sheet to run before the new slant of wind, the jib was drawing again. They passed the home dock, close in, came about and made a landing just as the first big drops of rain began to fall.

Luke got the sails off the boat as fast as he could, folded them and made the *Tern* fast to her moorings. He had to leave her there until later if he hoped to get the sails under cover before they were too wet.

At least, he told himself that night as he thought over his experience, it had taught him something about thunder squalls. You could expect a counter-clockwise shift in the wind. He mentioned it to his mother next morning and was surprised when she nodded knowingly.

"Of course," she told him with a smile, "I found that out a long time ago. Why do you suppose I always shut the west windows when it thunders in the north?"

*　　*　　*

The opening race of the season would be on May 30th, Memorial Day, and Luke wanted very much to be in it. There were some preliminary matters to be taken care of first. The membership in the Yacht Club given him by his father for Christmas was a help. But he had to be a member of the International Comet Class Yacht Racing Association, as well. His five-dollar dues were sent in and he got his membership card a few days before Memorial Day. Meanwhile he persuaded Axel Gundersen to become an associate member, so that he could race as a crew man. The rules were strict on that point, and since the dues came to only a dollar, Axel was happy to do it.

The next thing was to present his credentials to the Race Committee. He sailed down to the Yacht Club the Saturday before the race, carrying his certificates of membership, the registration of the *Tern*, and everything else he thought might be useful.

Marley Evans, skipper of the *Gull*, had been elected Commodore that year. He was one of the pioneers of Comet sailing on the coast and took a strong interest in the class. The chairman of the Race Committee was a short, stout individual named Cobley, a stranger to Luke.

Evans recognized the boy when he came in and offered his hand with a smile of welcome. Cobley seemed less cordial. When Luke laid his papers on the table and explained that he wanted to enter his boat, the chairman cleared his throat.

"Well, now," he said officiously, "it may not be as easy as all that. There are several requirements, you know. Are you a member of the Comet Association in good standing?"

Luke pointed to the card, then produced his other certificates. The fat man hemmed and hawed, put on his glasses and studied everything with a suspicious eye while Evans sat by, silently chuckling.

"Hm," said Cobley at last. "Everything seems to be in order. Three-oh-nine-five. Haven't I seen that boat number before?"

"I expect so," the boy replied. "She used to belong to Mr. Holliger."

"So? Then how'd you come to get her?"

Marley Evans leaned forward in his chair. "I know about that," he said quietly. "The boat broke loose from her moorings in the storm last fall, and was blown clear across the bay into the marsh. This lad salvaged the wreck and bought it from Holliger. From what I hear, he's done a nice job of repairing and refinishing, and I'm mighty glad he wants to race. That's what we need—more young people taking up sailing."

"Oh, of course," said Cobley hastily. "Sure—you're right, Commodore. I just remembered that number and was curious. You're sure you have all the necessary equipment, Cramer, and she's in proper condition to race?"

Luke tried to keep his temper. "I think so," he answered. "She's right here, tied up to the dock. You might take a look."

Evans smiled and got up. "Good idea," he said. "I'd like to see what you've done to her."

They went down the steps and out on the dock. Bunkie was lying close to the bollard where the painter was made fast. Now he rose, his tail wagging, and sniffed at Cobley's legs. The Race Committee chairman drew back in alarm.

"Wait a minute," he said. "I don't like dogs. Where'd he come from?"

"He's my crew," Luke said, grinning. "Here, boy, heel!"

"You mean you plan to race with that brute in the boat? It's against the rules."

"No," said the boy. "Axel Gundersen's going to crew for me. He's a qualified Associate Member of the Association. Now if you'll look her over—"

He pointed out the new anchor and line, stowed in the bow along with the kapok cushions. And try as he would, Cobley could find nothing to criticize.

Marley Evans ran an appreciative hand over the deck finish. "Beautiful!" he murmured. "If you handle her right she ought to be pretty fast. I can see I'll have to keep an eye on the *Tern* when we're in a race together."

When Luke got home he found a letter waiting for him. "I know you'll be in the Memorial Day race," Marilyn wrote, "and I'd give anything to be there. As a matter of fact I would if I didn't have to bone up for two exams the next day. School won't be over till the middle of June but we'll be coming down right after that. Do your best, Luke, and I'll keep my fingers crossed for you."

9

Memorial Day fell in the middle of the week. On Monday Luke boarded the school bus and found Johnny Grasso saving a seat for him. He had been a little worried about hurting Johnny's feelings by his choice of a crew man. Johnny was a good guy and quick to learn, but he didn't have the instinct for sailing that seemed to come naturally to Axel. Perhaps it took a heritage of generations of Norse seafarers to give a boy the kind of sailing judgment Axel had.

Johnny, however, was far from showing bitterness this morning. As usual he was full of news.

"Got me a summer job," he announced proudly. "Bus boy in the Yacht Club dining room. It's just weekends and holidays but I get good wages an' a share in the tips. I'll be startin' Memorial Day."

Luke congratulated him. "What do you hear about Holliger?" he asked. "Will his new boat be ready for this first race?"

"I guess not," said Johnny. "It's all straightened out with the Rules Committee, but there's some hold-up in gettin' the sails finished. He'll probably have her down here in a couple o' weeks. How 'bout you? You all set?"

Luke nodded. "I had a little trouble with that Mr. Cobley, but Marley Evans smoothed him down."

"That so-an'-so!" Johnny snorted. "You know who he is, don't you? Old Man Holliger's stooge! He got him appointed an' believe me he'll make it as tough as he can for all the other skippers."

That explained some of the things that had had Luke wondering. The Race Committee chairman's crusty attitude wasn't directed at him alone, as it had seemed.

Those last two days really dragged. Every evening after school, Luke toiled over the boat, polishing paint, tightening stays, or oiling sheaves. He worried about the weather, too. There was a cold front coming through, and a threat of showers. They arrived late in the afternoon of the day before the race and in their wake left cool, clear air and a brisk northwest breeze.

The holiday dawned fair. Axel came down early and they got the *Tern* in the water by ten. There would be two Comet races, the first starting at eleven, the second at three in the afternoon. They sailed down the bay to the club and Luke went ashore to study the course. A dozen other skippers were clustered around the bulletin board and he saw several he knew. Bruce Canning gave him a cordial greeting.

"A big day for you!" said the real estate man. "Here's luck in your first race!"

Luke was introduced to some of the others—all local people and most of them older than himself. The school and college group wouldn't be out in force till June.

The morning race was to be two laps around a five-mile triangle, starting south from the clubhouse, then westward for a mile or so, and a northeasterly slant back to the mark. In the afternoon they would be sailing the longer course, with a two-mile dog-leg deep into Dutchman's Bay.

He came out and reported these facts to Axel, who had been minding the boat. They checked on the direction of the wind. It was holding steady from a little north of west.

84

"We'll have it on our beam at first," said Luke. "Then we'll be beating into it on the short leg, and come home with the breeze off our port quarter."

The yellow flag that marked the starting line was now set out, a hundred yards or so from the clubhouse dock. Up on the deck where the judges sat, a bustle of activity could be seen, and Mr. Cobley was in the middle of it.

Luke grinned. "Come on," he said, "let's get out o' here an' take a warm-up cruise. My watch says ten-thirty-two. I'll set it to the second when they give us the preliminary gun, but we've got time for a little sailing."

They tacked out across the bay and were part way back when the ten-minute gun sounded. Luke set the sweep second hand on his watch. He could count nearly a dozen Comets circling to the north of the line, and two more came out of the basin by the time they got the five-minute signal. Luke jockeyed back and forth, keeping an occasional eye on the time. There was no count-down, but according to his five-ninety-eight watch he still had about forty seconds. Not wanting to go over the line too soon, he kept back beyond most of the others. What he wanted to do was get up good headway in the last three or four seconds and cut inside the marker on the windward side of the fleet.

"Better get up there," Axel warned, and Luke was just starting to say there was plenty of time when the gun roared above them. They would have been last over if one other boat hadn't crossed too early and been called back.

Luke swallowed his chagrin and gave all his attention to getting the most out of the *Tern*. She spread her wings and flew down the bay, moving handsomely, gaining on the rearmost boats.

"What the heck?" the young skipper growled at last. "Why'd he want to fire that gun four whole seconds early?"

Axel chuckled. "You set your watch by the *sound* o' the gun, didn't you?" he said. "An' weren't we more'n half a mile up the bay? Sound travels what—close to eleven hundred feet a second? Next time we'd better stay where we can *see* the signal."

"I'll be darned!" Luke answered with a sheepish grin. "That's what happened, all right. Well, I learned my lesson."

He had watched enough races to know that the first leg of the course usually separated the sheep from the goats. By the time the south buoy was reached, five sloops were closely bunched in the lead. Then there was a wide gap and a second group of four. The remaining five boats were strung out and straggling. Luke was sailing the *Tern* with all the skill he possessed and her response made him proud. In those first two miles they had passed all the other tailenders and were gaining on the second string.

Two Comets, right ahead, were luffing as they tried to outsmart each other on the turn. Joyfully, Luke cut over to leeward, passed the marker wide, and brought the helm up as he trimmed the sheet.

"Nice goin', boy!" cried Axel. He was hiked far out as the *Tern* heeled over on the starboard tack. Now that they were sailing close to the wind the set of the sails counted, and Luke tightened the outhaul a trifle, trying to get the sail as flat as possible. The time he had spent in polishing the hull proved its value now. The *Tern*, always fast on the wind, was outdoing herself.

"Ready to come about!" Luke yelled. They were even with the seventh boat now, and he knew if they could save a second or two in tacking, they would have her. Axel moved as smoothly as a big cat and the sloop scarcely broke stride as she heeled to starboard.

"Golly!" called the Norwegian boy. "I bet there isn't a boat on the bay can take this baby against the wind!"

86

Luke nodded, but he was still concentrating on the job ahead. He had his boat in seventh place now. With a lot of luck he might overtake number six by the time they got back to the end of the first lap.

The luck wasn't forthcoming. The other sloop turned the west buoy five lengths in the lead, and a fluke in the breeze came just as Luke started his jibe. The *Tern* hung there and lost headway. When she was finally around and her sails drawing, the boat ahead had picked up another three lengths.

"Rig the whisker pole," said Luke. "We may catch up on her a little if we run wing-and-wing."

With the mainsail out to starboard and the jib to port, the *Tern* hustled after the sixth Comet. The wind was too light to make her plane, but she gained, foot by foot. The tide was nearly at flood, and it helped rather than hindered them on this leg. Meanwhile they were far enough ahead of the trailing boats to have no worries about being passed.

Luke was within three lengths of the Comet ahead when he approached the clubhouse turn and got ready to cut around the buoy. A few cheers came to his ears but he was too busy at the moment to pay any attention. Like a well-oiled machine his crew man moved forward and snatched out the whisker pole at the second when Luke put his helm down. They whipped around the buoy and heeled over with sails trimmed on the port tack.

Looking ahead, they could see the leaders halfway down the reach. But closer—only two lengths ahead now—was the blue-painted Comet in sixth place.

That blue boat was well sailed. When Luke drew right astern of her to windward, her skipper luffed just enough to force the *Tern* to luff too. That was no good. It was putting them too far to windward of the mark. Disgustedly Luke brought his helm up and sailed to leeward. A hundred yards from the buoy the other skipper, still jockeying,

fell off to force him into a wide turn. That was just what Luke had been hoping he would do. Like lightning he jammed the tiller down, trimmed the main sheet, and cut inside his opponent. He had an overlap and sea room now, and he knew enough about racing rules to be sure he had the right of way.

The man at the helm of the other boat knew it too. He grinned and waved as Luke slipped through the opening, missing the marker by a couple of yards. Then the *Tern* rounded into the breeze and whisked away on her beat to the westward.

Axel was crouched low along the gunwale, trying to give as little wind resistance as possible. From his forward position he could see ahead, under the foot of the jib.

"Hey!" he yelled suddenly. "More wind comin'!" And as he pointed, Luke saw the darkening ruffle on the water. The five leading boats would have felt it first, but they were closer to the west side of the bay, where they were somewhat in the lee of the land. The freshening of the breeze at this point was all in the *Tern's* favor.

Luke was determined she should make the most of it. Like Axel, he lay out almost parallel with the waves, holding the boat on course by the tip end of the tiller extension. She fairly flew through the water. When they came about, halfway to the west marker, the first Comet had not yet made the turn and the other four leaders were strung out over a distance of nearly a quarter of a mile.

Luke knew he had no chance of winning, but at least he meant to catch up with the first flight if he could. The way his boat was pointing made it look possible. He tacked once more, a hundred yards from the buoy, and got into good position for the turn. When they rounded and spread their sails wing-and-wing for the run home, they were only two lengths behind the fifth Comet.

The wind had stayed strong. Axel took one look at the

way the seas creamed past and scrambled aft, close to Luke. Without an order he raised the centerboard. The bow lifted a little and the boat began to plane. One by one they could see the other sloops ahead of them set their jibs opposite the mainsails, until all five were running "wung-out."

That battle for fifth place was something Luke wouldn't forget for a long time. He sat tense, trying not to clutch the tiller too hard, leaning forward from time to time as if his body-English could push the boat on faster. He hadn't paid much attention to the Comet he was trying to catch. Now it suddenly dawned on him that she was his one-time favorite, the *Sally C*.

Bruce Canning wasn't looking back. He and his crew— another man his own age—were sailing with grim concentration. It was only when the *Tern* pulled right abeam that Canning glanced over, saw Luke and gaped in surprise.

"All right, son!" he called, laughing. "You haven't taken us yet!"

He beckoned the crew man farther aft and the *Sally C* also lifted her forefoot and planed. That was how they raced, head and head, right to the finish. If anything, the *Tern* gained a trifle. But the final leg came in on a slant from the southwest and the line had been placed squarely east and west. Canning, keeping his position to port, had the advantage, and there was little Luke could do about it. He stayed as close to his rival as he was able, but the *Sally C's* nose was a foot or two in front when they crossed.

There was plenty of cheering from the crowd on the dock and the clubhouse porch, for everyone had been watching that fight for fifth place. The winning Comet had crossed the line only twenty seconds ahead of them, and the next three boats had followed at brief intervals. When Luke had moored the *Tern* in the basin he found half a dozen yachtsmen waiting to congratulate him. Canning was one of the first.

"Boy, you threw a scare into me!" he said. "As a matter of fact it should have been a tie. One of the judges wanted to call it that, but Cobley overruled him. Anyhow, pulling up from thirteenth after a bad start is glory enough for any skipper. From now on I'll know yours is one boat to watch."

Luke grinned at the praise. "Thanks a lot," he answered. "We'll be trying harder this afternoon."

10

The two boys went to a nearby drugstore for lunch. When they had finished their hamburgers and shakes it was one-thirty. They entered the clubhouse, waved to Johnny Grasso, who was helping clear off the luncheon tables, and took a look at the chart for the afternoon race.

It would be over almost the same course that Luke had sailed the previous Labor Day. If the breeze didn't shift, it would involve more work to windward than in the morning.

"That suits me fine," Luke told Axel. "I've got a hunch this boat does best on the wind, and if we can tack as fast as we did this morning, we'll save a couple of seconds every time we come about."

"I reckon you're right," the Norwegian boy agreed. "How's the tide goin' to be?"

"Running out. That means it'll be against us at the start and helping on the way back. And speaking of starts, I aim to get across a whole lot quicker than I did in that first race."

Johnny Grasso came over, wiping his hands on a napkin. "Hi," he said. "I hear you did all right this mornin'. Say— young Mert Holliger just got in. Guess he drove that Caddy down from school. I heard him tell somebody his new boat'll be delivered next week. Well—got to run now or the head waiter'll jump me."

It promised to be a good afternoon for sailing. The breeze held steady and the sun was bright and hot. A few clouds were blowing up from the southwest but they were light and fleecy and held no threat of rain. At two-thirty the boys made sail once more and cast off to come out into the bay.

They sailed close to the Yacht Club dock on the port tack. Just as they passed it Luke heard a loud voice above him. He was hidden by the leech of the sail, but he would have recognized the voice anywhere.

"Hey, look-it," Mert Holliger was saying. "Number three-oh-nine-five! That's my old boat, fixed up with a homemade paint job. I sailed her for a couple o' years. Never liked her very much, though. Wait till you see the new Comet I've got comin'!"

Axel grinned at Luke. "Braggin' to the girls as usual," he said.

Luke stole a quick glimpse back at the dock. Mert had his back to them as he described the wonders of his new boat. He looked even bigger, handsomer, and more self-satisfied than ever. For a moment Luke thought one of the two girls with him was Marilyn, but a second glance showed it was someone else, pink and giggly.

"Shouldn't wonder if you'd be sailin' against him by the Fourth o' July," Axel remarked gravely.

Luke wrinkled his nose. "Yeah," he said. "I can hardly wait."

They tacked south for nearly a mile, but allowed plenty of time to get back. Luke meant to be close to the starting line when the ten-minute signal was raised. There were more Comets out that afternoon—a field of sixteen boats, all milling about near the clubhouse. It wasn't going to be easy to make a fast start.

"Which side o' the line do you figure'll be best?" asked Axel.

The young skipper checked on the wind again before he answered. It was still from the southwest, steady but not very strong.

"Close to the windward buoy, I guess," he replied finally. "With that jam, there won't be much chance of breaking through to leeward."

He kept an eye on his watch and on the upper deck of the clubhouse. This time he saw the big white disc go up. The gun sounded at almost the same instant. His sweep second hand was right on the dot.

There was a temptation, in those last minutes, to get up close to the line in the huddle of other sloops. He resisted it, tacking off to the west as the five-minute gun boomed. At last, when Axel had begun to grow fidgety, he swung over and coasted back, with the mainsail to starboard and no strain on the sheets. His watch said half a minute to go, and the western line marker was a little over a hundred yards away.

"Okay," he told Axel grimly, "here we go, an' I sure hope we don't cross too soon."

He trimmed the main sheet and eased the helm over. There was still open water at the windward end of the line, but several boats were tacking back that way. In the last five seconds one of them cut across his bows and he had to fall off to keep from a collision.

"Whang!" went the gun and they sailed over the line in the first flight. The Comet that had crossed in front of them had to come about to get inside the buoy and was left several lengths astern.

The *Tern* was to windward of all the others in the group. Her sails blanketed those of the nearest sloop and she slipped out a length in front. But over to leeward some of the experienced sailors were footing fast. Three or four,

Luke thought, were a shade ahead of him. He settled down to racing.

It was at the north buoy, two miles up the bay, that the pattern of the race began to show. Marley Evans's *Gull* rounded the marker first, with the *Sally C* close at her heels. Three other Comets were only a few lengths behind. Then came the *Tern*, well up in the first flight, and after a long gap the rest of the fleet lay trailed out astern.

They came about, rounding the buoy smartly. Heading into Dutchman's Bay, all the leaders were close-hauled on the port tack. Luke followed suit, for he knew that if the wind shifted it was likely to become more southerly. In any case it looked as if they could make the whole distance to the outer mark without coming about.

Right ahead and a little to windward was the blue Comet Luke had beaten that morning. He was gaining on her now, only about three lengths astern. Then suddenly he saw a flutter in the jib and in the luff of the mainsail. The *Tern* lost way.

"Hey!" Axel called. "What's up—did we hit a flaw?"

Luke's answer was to bring the helm up. "We're going to tack," he growled. Slowly the sloop responded and the breeze filled her sails again as she headed for the south shore of the bay.

"All right," Luke said. "Ready to come about again."

When they had squared away once more on the port tack he looked at his crew man with a sheepish grin. "I got caught flat-footed," he said. "Moved up close enough so we got back-winded."

He had sailed right into the blue boat's blanketing cone —the area of turbulent air that extends aft and to leeward of any close-hauled yacht. Getting out of it had cost him four precious lengths and he was ashamed of himself.

Now, however, they were far enough to windward to be safe, and the *Tern* was scudding along valiantly. She had

95

picked up a little of her loss when they reached the buoy. They rounded it, made a fast, smooth jibe, and set off in pursuit of the blue Comet with the wind abeam.

This time Luke was thinking. He remembered some of the diagrams he had seen in books and the advice he had heard from Bruce Canning. If he sailed right he might give the skipper ahead some of his own medicine. Halfway up the reach he was only two lengths astern of the blue boat and deliberately bore out to windward, gaining a little in speed. He had half expected his opponent to luff with him, but the other craft didn't change course.

Gradually the *Tern* pulled up on her starboard quarter. Luke watched the blue Comet's sails and saw what he had hoped for. There was a shaking in the leech of the mainsail. Hastily the other skipper bore off, trying to get out of the blanketing cone, but he was too late. The *Tern* drew even, then nosed past. She was in fifth place now.

"Nice goin'," said Axel with a grin. "You learn quick, don't you?"

"He helped me," Luke replied. "Guess he wasn't looking, or he could have luffed out of it while he was still in front."

They were past the mouth of Dutchman's Bay and running for the north buoy, with the fourth place Comet five or six lengths ahead. From the number on the sail Luke recognized it as a boat belonging to Jim Akins, a Philadelphia advertising man who summered on the island, known as a pretty good skipper. Any attack he made would have to wait for the beat down the bay.

"Ready to round the buoy!" he called. "An' let's make it one of our good ones!"

They turned the mark in snappy fashion, picking up a length. Instead of coming about they stayed on the starboard tack like the rest of the leaders. Luke had been expecting a shift of wind. Now, sure enough, it came—a puff right out of the south that ruffled the taut jib.

Before he could lose way the boy jammed the tiller over. "Ready about!" he yelled, and Axel ducked the boom in time.

They were the first to tack, though the boats in front must have felt the change at least as soon as they had. The wind was coming stronger now, and the *Tern*, heeled far over to starboard, was footing like a deer. Watching the leaders, Luke saw the third-place Comet get into trouble. The tack had brought her around close behind the *Sally C* and now she was blanketed. Before she could escape, Akins's boat had passed her and the *Tern*, well out to leeward, was gaining on her fast.

The tide had turned and was ebbing, moving down the bay in the direction they were sailing. Luke knew it ran strongest in mid-channel. He decided to tack again and take advantage of the current. Short tacks might lose headway for a boat that was slow coming about, but he figured he and Axel could do it as fast as anyone in the fleet.

They were close enough to the four boats ahead to see what was going on. Evans was trying to shake the *Sally C* off his tail by luffing, and each time he did it both boats lost way. As a consequence the third and fourth Comets were creeping up, with the *Tern* close behind them.

With the wind almost dead ahead as they neared the south mark, the approach tack became important. Luke had kept well out to the west, making sure he wouldn't be blanketed. When he was almost abreast of the buoy he brought her over fast so as to cut the mark close, with the wind on his starboard beam. The number four boat, still on the port tack, reached the turn at almost the same time.

"Hey!" her skipper yelled. "Give us buoy room!"

"Starboard tack!" Luke shouted back. "Stay clear—it's our right o' way!"

There was no question about it. The other sloop had to fall off to keep out of a collision, and by the time she had come about Luke had a two-length lead. He whipped around in a hundred-and-eighty-degree turn.

"Wing-an'-wing!" he called to Axel. In a jiffy the crew man had spread the jib to starboard and hustled aft to join him. They passed the clubhouse solidly in fourth place and only a short length astern of the blue boat. But try as he would, Luke was unable to gain before the wind. It wasn't until they were nearing the north buoy that he had a chance to blanket his opponent's mainsail. And that was only for a moment, because both Comets had to jibe to make the turn.

With Axel handling the jib and centerboard, Luke brought the boom over in a hurry. The sail filled away with a bang as he trimmed the sheet and put the helm down. By a second or two he beat the blue Comet in the maneuver. Cutting close to the mark, he was inside and right abeam of the other boat, taking the wind out of her sails. And by the time both were squared away on the port tack he had nosed in front.

Deep into Dutchman's Bay they were still in the same order—the *Gull* first, Canning close behind her, and the *Tern* holding third, three or four lengths astern. They made the west marker, came about and headed east again with the wind abeam.

"Breeze is gettin' fluky," Axel commented. "Blows in little puffs. You think it's goin' to shift again?"

Luke had noticed the change. Now he glanced at the sky in the north. It was hazy but there were no cumulus clouds.

"Hard to say," he answered. "We'll just have to play it by ear."

They came out of Dutchman's Bay for the last time, reached for the northern marker and made the swing around it without any change in position. On the beat down channel Luke knew he had his final chance to gain.

Once more he used short tacks, keeping near the middle, where the tide would help most. But Evans and Canning knew the bay as well as he did, and both boats were fast on the wind. He thought he picked up a yard or two each time he tacked, though there still seemed to be a lot of water between him and the *Sally C*.

The sudden shift of wind caught all three boats off guard. Luke felt it first in the slacking of the sheet. There was a moment of dead calm, then a sharp gust out of the east. Luckily the *Tern* was on the port tack and she heeled over till the sea was almost in the cockpit. Canning, on the opposite tack, was taken full aback and his forestay snapped with a *ping* they could hear plainly.

"Tough luck for him," shouted Axel, as he hiked far out over the weather gunwale. "But we've got second place if nothin' happens to us."

Luke had no time to answer. He was too much occupied keeping the sloop on her course, which had now become a close reach. With the disabled *Sally C* far astern, he was three lengths back of the leader when they approached the south buoy.

He waited till he was sure he could clear it, then came about with a rush. With the wind strong on the starboard beam, he settled down for the final dash to the finish line.

There was a lot of noise up ahead—a honking of horns and cheering from the clubhouse. Through the window in the sail he saw the *Gull* bear off suddenly and realized she had done it to keep from running down the crippled *Sally C*. Then his heart leaped, for he knew he had his chance.

The *Tern* was far enough to windward to clear Canning's sloop and still hold her course for the line! She was almost even with the first-place Comet now.

"Come on, baby," Luke muttered through clenched teeth. "Do your prettiest—go—go!"

As if she heard him and answered, the boat seemed to fly faster. And the Yacht Club dock was very close. Through the drumming in his ears Luke heard an excited bellow over the loudspeaker.

"Three-oh-nine-five, over!" it said. Then, without pause, "Three-oh-oh-one—over!"

"You hear that?" Axel yelled. "We won! Less'n half a length, but we crossed first!"

Luke was almost too dazed to take it in at first. Then he shook his head in wonder. "You're right," he said in a shaky voice he hardly recognized as his own. "We really did it!"

11

Luke didn't hang around the clubhouse long after the race. He was tired. Physically and mentally he had been under tension for hours, and he needed to get away by himself, where he could unwind. There were plenty of people who wanted to congratulate him. The younger local sailors in particular seemed to feel he was their hero. However, he had no illusions. The *Tern* had proved herself, and with the help of some luck he thought he had sailed her well enough. But when the regular summer season started and the real pros arrived, he knew the competition would get a lot tougher.

One of those who had shaken his hand on the dock was Mert Holliger. The heir to the Haulfast fortune was still a bit condescending, but he obviously had more respect for Luke as a future opponent. He looked the boat over speculatively, as if he was wondering what had been done to add to her speed.

When he left, Axel chuckled. "Guess you gave him quite a jolt," the young Norwegian commented. "He didn't even brag about his own new boat!"

The next evening, feeling more relaxed, Luke returned to the clubhouse to see if the point ratings had been posted. They were there on the bulletin board. Marley Evans, who had won the morning race and come in so close to him in the afternoon, was at the top of the list with 27¼ points. And in second place appeared his own name—"Luke Cramer, *Tern*, No. 3095—22¼ points." The scoring included one point for each boat beaten, plus a quarter-point for a win.

He stopped at Bruce Canning's house on the way home. The real estate man was working on the *Sally C*, putting on a new set of stays all around, but he stopped to give Luke a warm handshake.

"As long as I was out of it," he said, "I was sure tickled to see you come through. That forestay had been on too long, and I knew it. If I'd been on the other tack I expect everything would have held, but anyhow I got my warning and I'm glad it was early in the season. Next time, look out!"

"That was an awfully tough piece of luck," Luke told him. "Tough on Mr. Evans, too, because I'd never have caught him if he hadn't borne off to keep from hitting you."

Canning nodded. "Maybe. It would have been close, though. By the way, won't you be graduating from high school in a week or two? What are your plans? Want to go to college?"

"I'd like to," said Luke. "I've sent my application to Rutgers. My grades have been pretty good, and I ought to get in. But I'll need a little more money than Dad can afford right now."

"Good—that's exactly what I was coming to. If you don't have a summer job lined up, how'd you like to work for me? This is going to be a big season—more things to do than I can handle alone. You make a good impression on people, and you could be a lot of help, showing properties, and so on. I think," Canning added with a smile, "we'd be able to arrange our working hours so we'd both have time for sailing."

"Gosh!" said Luke, delighted. "I don't know anybody

I'd rather work for. If you really mean it I'm saying yes quick, before you can change your mind."

He hurried home to tell his family the good news and found them as pleased as he was.

"The pay'll be better than I could give you for clerking in the store," his father said. "And real estate's a good business to be in, down here. Bruce Canning can teach you a lot, and he's a first-class citizen."

Those last days of school went by in a whirl. Graduation came on a Wednesday. Attired in his best clothes, Luke sat through the final exercises and the long Commencement harangue made by a state senator. Then he went up for his diploma, and endured the reception outside in the heat afterwards.

What saved the occasion was looking forward to the Senior party that night. They had it on the beach, with a moon and a bonfire, hot dogs and cokes, and a portable record-player that gave them the background music for dancing, swimming, and romance. The party didn't break up till the red rim of a rising sun appeared out of the sea, and Luke slept most of the following day.

Friday he went to work, feeling mature but well-rested. Dressed in a clean sport shirt, jacket, and slacks, he arrived at the office promptly at eight. Canning wasn't there yet. However, Luke had the key and let himself in. He swept the floor, emptied the ash-trays, and tidied up the desk and the counter. Mrs. Cramer had made him bring a bouquet of her nicest roses, and he found a vase for them. By the time his boss arrived the place had a gay look and smelled like a flower garden.

"Whew!" Canning whistled. "Is this where I work? Thank your mother for me, Luke, and let's hope none of the customers have rose fever."

He kept the boy busy that morning, familiarizing himself with the list of houses available. Luke went out for lunch at the drugstore at noon, and when he came back the office was full of would-be renters from the city, who had taken Friday afternoon off. Bruce Canning called him aside.

"I've got my hands full here," he said. "I want you to run down to the Haven and get a place ready for some important clients. They've taken that big cottage on the Beach Road at Crow's-Nest Point, and they'll be coming this afternoon. Here are the keys. Make sure the screens are up, the windows open, and the electricity and water turned on."

Luke got on his bicycle and rode the two miles down the island. He knew the house—one of the older show-places, built back in the lush twenties. It was a big, sprawling, comfortable house, with wide verandas and a magnificent view of the ocean.

He unlocked the front door, tried the light switches, and turned on a faucet or two. Everything was working properly. The house had been cleaned and the screens were in place. All he had to do was to go around opening windows, so that it would be cool and airy when the tenants arrived.

Luke was in one of the bedrooms on the second floor when he heard the crunching of tires on the driveway gravel. He hurriedly opened a final window and was starting down the stairs when he heard a gay voice below.

"Look, Mother—isn't it a dream? And all opened up, ready for us!"

He knew that voice and his heart skipped a beat. Why hadn't Canning told him it was the March family that was expected?

Marilyn heard his step on the stairs and looked up, her face suddenly changing color. "Why—why, Luke!" she exclaimed. "How wonderful! Did you know we were coming? Mother, this is Luke Cramer—you remember?"

Mrs. March acknowledged the introduction graciously. She was, Luke thought, almost as attractive as her daughter in a more mature way.

"I didn't know it would be you," he stammered. "You see I'm working for Mr. Canning this summer and he just sent me down to be sure everything was ready here. But, golly, Marilyn, I'm glad to see you! If there's anything you want done, Mrs. March, let me know. Maybe I can bring the luggage in for you."

Mrs. March smiled. "That's nice of you," she said, "but I'm sure Michael and Frieda can manage."

At that moment a uniformed chauffeur and a sturdy German maid appeared on the front porch, loaded down with bags. Luke hurried to open the screen door for them.

"We're going to have lunch in a few minutes," said Marilyn. "Why don't you stay and eat with us? I'm wild to hear all about the *Tern*."

Luke shook his head. "Thanks," he answered, "but I've already had lunch. And now you're here I ought to get back. You see, this is my first day and I'd better stay on the ball. Tell you what, though. If you'd like to go for a sail I'll bring the boat down and pick you up any evening. I get off at five and I could be at your dock by six-thirty."

Marilyn beamed. "Wonderful!" she said. "Let's make it tonight. I'm crazy to see her. Is it a date?"

"Sure is." Luke grinned as he got on his bicycle.

He was given plenty to do the rest of the afternoon, but shortly after five he was pedaling home. He changed to sailing clothes, ate a hasty supper and got the Comet in the water. Right at the appointed time he was tied up at the pier, across the island from Crow's-Nest Point.

Marilyn was only a few minutes late—really prompt for a girl, he thought. She drove over in the Thunderbird, dressed in dungarees and a pink sweater. There was a scarf over her hair, for the breeze blew strongly out of the southeast.

"Hi," she called gaily, "did you think I was going to stand you up? Mother insisted I help Frieda with the dishes. I told you there was no spoiling in my family."

She stood on the dock and looked over the *Tern*. "Luke," she said, "you've got the prettiest boat on the bay! She's lovely. How did you do in the Memorial Day races?"

He gave her a hand down into the cockpit and cast off. "Well," he said, when they were clear, "I guess I had an awful lot of luck—after a miserable start in the morning."

As they ran before the wind he told her what had happened in both races, careful not to do any boasting.

"The *Tern*'s fast, all right," he concluded. "But I've still got a lot to learn before I get the most out of her. Axel helped. He's a crackerjack crew man—a natural sailor. You'll like Axel Gundersen."

She wrinkled her nose at him. "I guess I'm jealous of Axel," she said, "even when I'm sure he's your best racing crew. But you're going to teach me to sail—remember?"

"All right," Luke said, laughing. "Start now. Here's the tiller and the sheet."

She slipped past him into the helmsman's position and took her grip on the tiller. "Mm," she said. "This is fun!"

Luke gauged the distance to the west shore of the bay. "Pretty soon," he told her, "we'll have to come about. Know what to do?"

"I think so. Do you want to start tacking back, or shall we head down the bay on a close reach?"

The boy tried not to show his surprise. "Down the bay'll be fine," he answered. "I'll handle the jib. Say when."

"Now," she said. Expertly she eased the helm down and hauled the main sheet while Luke trimmed the jib. The *Tern* heeled on the port tack with both of them leaning far back against the breeze.

"This is what I love," said Marilyn. "And she is fast—just see her cut along!"

Luke looked at her reproachfully. "Well, young lady," he said, "you've got some explaining to do. Why didn't you tell me you were a real sailor?"

The girl laughed. "I'm not, as a matter of fact. A certain guy used to take me out in his boat, but he was such an expert he wouldn't let me touch anything. I watched what he did, though. Sometimes I thought I could do it better. Mert won't ever be really good at it until he gets over being so heavy-handed."

"I know what you mean," Luke told her. "You have to keep the feel of the boat or she won't give you her best. He may learn how, with this new Comet he's getting."

"Have you seen her yet?" Marilyn asked.

"Not yet. I'm not sure she's even been delivered."

"Yes," she said. "She's here, all right. I understand he took a trial sail this morning. They tell me she's a beautiful boat—green, of course."

Luke chuckled. "Of course. And I bet her name is something about 'Haulfast.'"

She didn't answer for a moment, and, though her face was turned away, he could see a flush creeping up her cheek.

"You'll know soon enough," she said at last. "And it makes me unhappy. He's calling her the *Marilyn*."

It was Luke's turn to be red-faced. "Is that so?" he asked, trying not to sound bitter. "I suppose that means you'll be sailing with him?"

"Oh, Luke, please try and understand. He didn't ask my permission—just went ahead and had the name painted on. He knew how angry I was last fall, but I suppose he simply took it for granted I'd get over it and we'd go around together this summer. An open break would make trouble. I mean—you know my father works for Mr.

Holliger. So I'll probably have to keep on seeing him. But please—you'll let me sail with you?"

"Sure," he said soberly. "Sure, Marilyn—any time you say. When I'm not working, that is."

Silent and troubled, she turned the tiller over to him and went forward to the crew position. At his order they came about shortly after, and made a broad reach of it back to the place they had started.

"It's been a beautiful evening," she said, when he gave her a hand up to the dock. "Sorry I spoiled it."

Then she was gone. On the sail homeward he had time to swallow his hurt pride. Perhaps he had been lucky in one way, at least. The thought of what would have happened if he hadn't resisted his first impulse in naming his boat made him squirm. But he couldn't find it in his heart to forgive Mert Holliger. That, he knew, was a score that sooner or later would have to be settled.

Luke got his first look at the new boat that weekend. There was no race scheduled, so on Sunday afternoon he took his young sister Joan out for a sail. Naturally she was delighted and obeyed all his commands with alacrity. He had to admit to himself, though he didn't tell her, that she had the makings of a pretty good crew.

They were cruising south, beating against a light breeze, when a shining new sail appeared among the cluster of others near the Yacht Club. The number sewed on it was new, too—3420.

"That boat looks almost like this one used to," Joan commented. "The same green color. Do you suppose it's Holliger's?"

"Shouldn't wonder," her brother replied curtly. He didn't pull over to investigate but held his course southward. It was twenty minutes later, when they came about for the run up the bay, that the green Comet swept past, close-hauled. Mert was at the helm and another youth, with a duck-tail haircut and long sideburns, sat beside him. They exchanged casual waves and drew rapidly apart.

"*Marilyn*," Joan read out. "Why—wasn't that the name of the girl who sent you—"

Luke's face was like a thundercloud, and when she saw it her voice faded out in the middle of her question.

"Well," she said at last, to break the heavy silence, "if that's Mert Holliger's wonderful glass boat, I don't think it's half as pretty as this one. I bet it won't go any faster, either."

Her brother gave her a grin that made her feel better. "Thanks, small fry," he said. "You're okay."

12

Luke rebounded quickly from the blow he had received. He liked working with Bruce Canning and he did his best to earn his pay. The first time he succeeded in renting a cottage he came home filled with pride. And when, a week later, he sold a small property, he felt he had really arrived in the real estate business.

Canning, in turn, depended on him more as the days passed, and gave him greater responsibility. His wages, plus commissions, in the first two weeks, amounted to over a hundred and seventy dollars.

Meanwhile he still saw Marilyn March occasionally, though less often than he would have liked. Several times she dropped in at the drugstore where she knew he ate lunch. Once she called him at the office and they made a date for another sail that evening. There was a little restraint between them still, though she tried to be as natural and friendly as ever. He couldn't help feeling that the girl really enjoyed being with him.

On the other hand he knew she spent a good deal of time in Mert Holliger's company. Mert had a new speed-boat this year—a semi-hydroplane with three-hundred-plus horsepower that was reputed to do sixty miles an hour. In it he delighted to roar up and down the bay with half a dozen of the younger summer crowd packed in the cockpit or clinging to the forward deck. Marilyn was often in the party. Once, when Luke had business at the clubhouse, he saw the two of them getting into the green Comet to go sailing. And he heard that Mert took her to the Saturday night Yacht Club dances.

The last weekend in June it was announced that there would be a local warm-up race for the big Fourth of July regatta, which would be held at Seaside Park. Because a number of members had missed the Memorial Day affair, the committee ruled that club points would be scored that Saturday.

Luke was ready. He called up Axel and got his promise to be on hand. The race wouldn't start till one, and Luke figured he could clean up the morning's work by twelve, in time to make the start. He knew Bruce Canning would like to be in it, too.

The blow fell at eleven-thirty that morning. Three carloads of people from Philadelphia pulled up in front of the office, all wanting cottages for July. There were only a few of the less desirable places still unrented, but possible business couldn't be turned away. With a heavy heart Luke took the assignment to guide one group, while Canning handled the others. Luke barely had time to call Axel, and was lucky to catch his crew man before he left.

It was nearly two o'clock when the job was finished. Luke's party of prospects had liked none of the houses he showed them and had gone on to another shore resort. Bruce Canning had managed to rent one small cottage.

He looked at his young assistant across the desk and gave him a one-sided grin. "Too bad," he said. "I owe you a lunch for that. Come on down to the Yacht Club with me and we'll watch those gentlemen of leisure race while we get something to eat."

Most of the home fleet was out that day. Twenty-two Comets had started and they were coming down for the end of the first lap when Luke and his companion reached the upper deck, overlooking the bay.

"Your eyes are better than mine," Canning said. "Who's in those three leading boats?"

Luke shaded his eyes against the sun. "Looks like Mr. Evans in first place. Yeah—that's three-oh-oh-one on the sail. I can't make out the next one's number, but she's painted yellow. Third is a green boat. Must be Mert Holliger's new fiberglas job."

There was a good sailing breeze from the west, and the three leaders were reaching for the south buoy closely bunched. The rest of the fleet was strung out over half a mile or more.

As they drew abreast of the clubhouse, Luke could see not only the sail numbers but even the faces of the crews. Holliger had his duck-tailed schoolmate, a boy named Lonny Sholtz, sailing with him. The yellow boat, Luke discovered from the list of registered numbers, belonged to a new member named Fawcett, who had transferred from Riverton Yacht Club, up on the Delaware.

"Our friend Holliger seems to have some speed," Canning observed as he munched a sandwich. "And look at the sweet set o' those sails! If he doesn't try anything fancy at the turn, he'll be in a good position to catch 'em on the second round."

Luke half expected Mert to pull a tricky maneuver as he had seen him do before. But either he had learned caution or he had supreme confidence in the speed of the *Marilyn.* He brought her around the marker in orthodox fashion, jibed smartly and lay over, close-hauled for the long leg up the bay.

They watched the rest of the boats make the turn, then went back to the dining room for pie à la mode and relaxed in the shade of the canopy to wait for the finish. Canning borrowed a good pair of binoculars from a friend and tried to make out the sails as the Comets beat westward into Dutchman's Bay.

"By golly!" he exclaimed. "I believe Holliger's taken over second now, and Marley's going to have to push the old *Gull* or he'll be passed, too!"

Luke groaned inwardly. He asked to take the glasses and focused them on the sails, half hidden behind the marsh grass. The shining white of Holliger's new canvas stood out, even though the number was obscured. He was in second place, all right. It looked as if he had passed Fawcett by a couple of lengths and was only about the same distance behind Evans. However, when boats were tacking it wasn't easy to be sure of their position. He could tell better when they came around to run out of the bay.

Canning laughed. "Looks as if we'd have some hot competition this summer," he said.

The rest of the fleet was in Dutchman's Bay now, and the tangle of crisscrossing sails made it impossible to tell what was happening. When the leaders cleared the entrance, however, they could see the green boat right on Evans's tail.

"He'll have a tough time if he's trying to steal Marley's wind," said Canning. "I've thought I could do it plenty of times, but the old fox was too smart for me."

The *Gull* held her scant lead to the north buoy, but as they came about for the final leg they appeared to be almost neck-and-neck. The crowd on the dock and the clubhouse porch watched intently and the excited talk rose in pitch.

"Well, well!" Luke heard a booming voice below. "That's *my* kid an' he's takin' the lead! Anybody got ten dollars says he won't win?"

It was Merton Holliger, Senior, strutting about the dock in a purple sport shirt, his chest puffed out like a pouter pigeon's. There were no takers apparently, though he offered to double the bet. It was fairly obvious by then that the green Comet was gradually pulling a little ahead of her rival.

But the "old fox" wasn't through yet. His *Gull* was in the windward berth and they could see her fall off slightly, bringing the two craft closer together. Holliger didn't seem to realize what was happening at first. Then he felt the effect of the other sloop's blanketing cone and he, too, swung off to port, trying to pull clear. It was too late. The white boat stuck to him like a leech, stealing his wind, making the *Marilyn's* mainsail flutter.

In desperation the younger skipper luffed, but he had already lost too much way. The *Gull,* with her sails still drawing full, shot out nearly a length in front. With only a hundred yards to the finish line, Evans managed to hold most of that lead, and there was no question which was the winning Comet.

Down on the dock the elder Holliger was red-faced but strangely quiet. Watching him, Bruce Canning chuckled.

"You see now," he told Luke, "why it isn't always the fastest boat that crosses first. The experience that comes with age is still worth something in sailing."

There was no race on Sunday. To Luke's great delight he got a call from Marilyn after church. She asked if he was taking the *Tern* out that afternoon and if she could go along. His answer, naturally, was that he'd be happy to have her.

The wind, as it often did in hot weather, had shifted before eleven o'clock and now blew cool and refreshing from the southeast. They sailed up the bay with the breeze over the starboard quarter.

Luke didn't like to bring up the subject of Saturday's race. Before long, however, Marilyn was talking about it.

She had been to the dance with Mert Holliger the night before.

"I hate a poor loser," she said, wrinkling her nose in distaste. "He spent half the evening blaming the fit of his sails. As if that had anything to do with it!"

"I thought they were perfect," Luke replied, puzzled. "Bruce Canning was admiring 'em, too. With all the speed he's got, I don't see how there can be anything wrong with the sails."

"Well," she said, "he's talking about getting the sail-maker down here—maybe ordering a new set."

Luke laughed. "When he's got twenty points on the board? Gosh, what's he want to do—miss out on some more races?"

"No indeed," said Marilyn. "He'll keep on racing with these while the new ones are being made. Oh, Luke—I hope you beat him! I was sorry you weren't in it yesterday."

"Thanks," he said. "So was I. I won't know whether this boat is quite as fast as his until we get together, but maybe Axel and I can at least keep him in sight. Are you going up to Seaside to watch the regatta?"

"I've been invited," she answered, looking away. "Mr. Holliger's taking us all up in his cabin cruiser. But you know I'll be pulling for you."

*　　*　　*

The Canning real estate office was to be closed all day on the Fourth. There would be two races, morning and afternoon, and at least seven boats from the Man-o'-War fleet were going north to compete.

The night before, Luke made all his preparations. The *Tern* was on her trailer, with a red flag on the butt of the unstepped mast. He had his trailer license and taillight, and he fastened the hitch to the rear bumper of the Buick, ready to make an early start. It had rained a little the first two days of the week. Now the weather forecasts promised sun and high temperatures for the holiday, with a chance of afternoon thundershowers.

Luke rose at six, too excited to eat much breakfast. He was still tense as he drove up the road, keeping an eye on the rear-view mirror to see how the trailer was towing. At the causeway he picked up Axel, who had arranged to meet him there.

The big Norwegian saw his serious face and laughed. "Take it easy, Luke," he said. "The boat's ridin' pretty, back there, an' we've got loads o' time. Once we're on the Garden State Parkway we'll be up there before you know it."

They reached the big toll road a few miles inland and headed north at a steady fifty miles an hour. That was under the speed limit, but Luke's mind was on the precious boat behind him. Other Comet trailers passed them from time to time. They were coming up the coast from Wildwood and Stone Harbor and Ocean City—the pick of the fleets.

A mile or two below the exit for Seaside Park a big Cadillac convertible whipped by, towing a boat that gleamed green in the sunshine.

"Holliger?" asked Axel.

Luke nodded. "I'm afraid you'll see a lot more o' that boat before the day's over. He came mighty close to winning last Saturday."

They unhitched the trailer as near the ramp at the Yacht Club as they could get. The space was already crowded with Comets, and more were arriving from moment to moment. Luke went in to report to the Race Committee and show his credentials. Bruce Canning was there before him. He introduced the boy to the officials, then drew him aside.

119

"Man-o'-War's chances are going to depend pretty heavily on you and Mert Holliger and myself," he told Luke. "Marley Evans won't be here—caught a bad cold Monday and he's in bed. There'll be thirty or thirty-five boats out, so I figure we're in for something of a rat-race, especially at the start. The course isn't particularly tricky, though. It's twice around a triangle—south, then a short leg west and a long one northeast to the starting point."

"How's the wind?" the boy asked. "Looks westerly to me."

"That's right, but it's liable to shift. And you may find it a bit flukier than down our way because these bluffs are higher. So keep an eye out for flaws. Let's get the boats in and cruise around a bit."

The sun on the water beat down hot and the air was heavy, even in the small shore breeze. Watching the lazy set of his sails, Luke was unhappy.

"Looks as if it might turn out to be a doggone drifting match," he growled to his crew man.

"Well," said Axel comfortingly, "everybody'll have the same wind. How do you know we can't drift just as fast as they can? I bet there are mighty few boats with any slicker bottom than this one."

The morning race was scheduled to start at ten-thirty because of the lightness of the breeze. Luke had set his watch by the clubhouse clock and at ten-twenty, when the warning signal went up, he was correct to the second. North of the starting line the Comets were swarming like bees around a hive.

As the minutes ticked away, the traffic jam grew worse. The outer buoy had been moved unusually far from the dock to give the fleet more room, but even so, Luke could see there was sure to be trouble. He kept the *Tern* well over to the windward, moving slowly on the port tack.

When there was one minute to go he brought her about.

His idea was to run along parallel with the line, the wind over his starboard quarter, then trim the sheet at the gun and go across. The strategy was sound except that at least ten other skippers were using it. Canning was one. He grinned across at Luke and shook his head ruefully.

When the red signal went up there was a hopeless tangle, with gunwales rubbing and sailors on the starboard tack yelling at those on the port tack to get out of the way. Nevertheless the start was allowed. Luke brought his helm up and bulled his way through the jam with close to a dozen boats ahead of him.

The southward reach was a slow business. The close-hauled Comets moved sluggishly through waves that were hardly more than ripples. Luke tried to keep over to windward, so as not to be robbed of such breeze as there was. He saw the *Sally C* a few lengths in front and to leeward, and well up among the leaders. The *Marilyn* was right abeam, for Holliger had made no better start than he had. Gradually the fleet began to string out. The newer boats and those with the smoothest paint drew away little by little from the pack. There was small chance for brilliant tactics unless the wind flawed or shifted.

Axel, watching the water like a hawk, warned him quietly that there was dead air ahead. "It's in the lee o' that bluff," he said. "Better fall off a bit."

Luke eased the helm down and slacked the sheet. He could see that most of the local skippers had kept off to leeward. But Mert Holliger, still close abeam, didn't understand the maneuver.

"What you tryin' to do—foul me?" he called angrily.

Luke pointed to the glassy water off the starboard bow. "No wind there," he replied. "We'll both be better off if we get over to leeward."

"Nothin' doin'! I'm stayin' where I am. An' don't think you can pull any o' your tricks on me."

All Luke could do was trim the sheet again to avoid a collision. "Okay," he called back. "Watch the boats go by. And don't say I didn't warn you."

Within two minutes both Comets were drifting in stagnant air while rivals passed them one after another.

"The pig-headed so-an'-so," Axel muttered. "Wonder how he likes it now!"

Luke didn't answer. He was watching the green boat's bow, and it was inching almost imperceptibly ahead.

13

It seemed like hours before they felt the wind again. Actually it was only five or six minutes, but by the time the gentle breeze bellied their sagging sails the *Marilyn* and the *Tern* were almost the last boats in the race. The green Comet had drifted just enough faster to be half a length ahead.

Grimly Luke bent to his sailing again. Thanks to young Holliger there was a lot of ground to make up. He looked up at the scarlet wind-sock and noticed that the breeze was shifting a little toward the south. That might mean it would grow stronger as well. Waiting till the green boat had pulled ahead a trifle farther, he let the *Tern* fall off and crossed astern of his rival, picking up a little speed in the process. In a moment he was safely through the blanketing cone and moving well to port with the wind right abeam.

As he had guessed, it began to blow harder and swung still farther into the south. The sloop heeled nicely, every inch of sail doing its job.

"I can count twenty-two boats in front of us," Axel announced. "Nine behind us now. An' one of 'em's green," he added with a grin.

The leaders had caught the freshening wind earlier and were making the most of it. The first flight had pulled a good half mile ahead of the *Tern*. But, Luke told himself, there was a lot of racing still to come. He held his course till he was sure he had a good lead on the *Marilyn*, then made a short beat to the westward, getting into position for a starboard tack that would take him straight down to the buoy.

He calculated it well. On the port tack he cut across Holliger's bows, then gave the order to Axel and came about fast. Settled away on the starboard tack once more, they were a little to windward of their rival and a good length in the lead.

Right ahead were five or six Comets, all trying to make more westing, all on the port tack. Having the right of way, Luke plowed through between two boats. Some of the others came about as soon as he had gone by, but he had headed them all. In addition he could see over his shoulder that they were making trouble for the closely pursuing *Marilyn*.

"Five down," his crew man called. "Seventeen to go."

By the time they neared the south mark, the scudding *Tern* had pulled up on another cluster of sloops, though the leaders had long since gone around and were headed well away on the windward leg. Four boats came down to the mark almost together, with Luke right at their heels. He made a tight, fast turn and came about immediately. Now that the rising breeze was south-southwest, he knew he could make the west buoy on a single close reach.

He slipped past two Comets, then a third. "Great goin'," Axel applauded. "But here comes Mert. He's really movin' too."

The green boat was a scant three lengths behind him. Gaining? No, Luke didn't think so. If she was faster than the *Tern*, close-hauled, somebody would have to prove it to him.

They began to meet the leaders, running up the bay on the third leg, full before the wind. Luke was glad to see the *Sally C* going well in third place. Ahead of her were a pair of sleek-looking Comets from other clubs.

When Luke approached the windward mark and prepared to jibe around it, he could count only nine boats ahead of him. And of those, two seemed to be well within striking distance. Meanwhile the green sloop was still there in his wake—still less than four lengths astern.

They cut the buoy close, made the jibe successfully and spread their wings full out. Axel raised the centerboard and scrambled aft. They were close enough now to steal some of the wind from the two boats ahead. Gaining, foot by foot, Luke pulled out a shade to windward to pass the first one. He got an overlap, drew even, and nosed ahead.

It was just at that moment that he felt the *Tern's* speed falter. There was an easing in the taut belly of the jib— the beginning of a flutter. With a quick glance astern he realized that the *Marilyn* had snaked up to within three lengths and was starting to blanket him.

Hastily he put the helm over and moved out farther to windward, trying to escape the smothering effect of the sails behind him. The jib filled again and the sloop began to plane. They were still running in ninth place. But now Holliger was close on their lee quarter.

Before they reached the clubhouse turn they had overtaken another sloop and were holding their short lead on the *Marilyn*. More than that, it was certain that they had gained some ground in their pursuit of the leaders. Yet neither Luke nor his crew man felt as jubilant about their progress as they might. The shadow of Mert Holliger's sail was too much of a threat.

With the centerboard down once more they rounded the buoy for the beat to the south. No longer was there dead water in the lee of the bluff. By pointing high, Luke thought he could make it in three tacks, and he had a sure confidence in the *Tern's* speed beating to windward. She proved him right. Heeled over clear to her gunwale, she raced down the bay on the starboard tack, pulling ahead of the *Marilyn* yard by yard.

When they went over on the port tack they had a full two lengths lead, and by the time they reached the south buoy it was three lengths. Axel could grin again.

"Let's take a couple more boats on this leg," he urged. "We're pullin' up on 'em."

Looking ahead, Luke could see that the leaders were still close-hauled on the reach to westward. Nearer to him were Fawcett's yellow sloop from Man-o'-War and a local Comet, fighting it out for sixth place. Fawcett had a slim lead. Even as the boys watched he luffed to port, forcing the other boat to luff with him, and both lost some headway. It looked like the opportunity the *Tern* had needed.

Luke brought the helm up gently, letting her bear away a little. In the next minute he had slipped through into the safe leeward position, with the spill of air off his close-trimmed mainsail back-winding the trailing sloop. At once Fawcett saw what was happening. He filled away on course again, raising a hand in salute to the *Tern*, now almost abreast.

"Guess he thinks you were just tryin' to help him," Axel laughed. "The old team spirit."

"Why not?" said Luke. "I don't mind picking up a point for a fellow member. Besides, I'm pretty sure we can outsail him on the last leg."

There was no chance to pass the yellow boat before they reached the mark. They came about on the inside, with a good overlap, and almost at once they pulled even. Looking over his shoulder, Luke saw the green hull of the

Marilyn making the turn. Holliger had hung doggedly to the chase. He was still only three lengths behind.

The centerboard was up now, and the *Tern* was "wung-out" for the last leg of the race. One thing Luke was determined to avoid. He wouldn't let the *Marilyn* blanket him this time. As soon as he was a length ahead of Fawcett he kept well over to starboard. It was a shade off course, but at least he could sail his own race without interference.

Holliger had Fawcett in his blanketing-cone now. The yellow boat lost way, pulled out of it as the *Tern* had on the first round, then steadied. But the *Marilyn* was too fast. She came bowling up to windward and left the yellow sloop astern.

It was a fight for fifth place now. The four leading boats were too far ahead to be caught. Luke watched his rival warily, for he had a hunch Holliger was going to try it again. Sure enough, the *Marilyn's* bow veered to starboard, toward his wake, and in the same instant Luke put his helm over, steering to port. It wasn't a real zigzag—just a tantalizing variation of course that kept the frustrated skipper of the *Marilyn* from stealing his wind.

They kept it up for another five minutes. Then the green Comet quit trying and sailed a straight course for the nearest finish marker. Luke relaxed and smiled at last. He knew he had the other boy licked.

Pleasure boats were jamming both sides of the course near the clubhouse, and the cheering reached them even in the teeth of the following breeze. With the first four Comets already in, the attention of the big crowd was on the *Tern* and the *Marilyn*.

"There's somebody waving at us," Axel announced. "A mighty pretty somebody, too!"

Luke saw her, high on the bow of the big mahogany

cruiser. He couldn't hear what she was shouting but there was no doubt about which boat she wanted to cross first. With two solid lengths to spare, the *Tern* scudded over the line.

❖   ❖   ❖

There was a buffet luncheon at the Yacht Club for the visiting skippers and crews. All sorts of seafood delicacies were spread temptingly on the long table, and Luke and Axel ate with good appetites and came back for more.

"It's a regular smorgasbord," the Norwegian boy commented with his mouth full of shrimp. "Trouble is, if I really let myself go, I'd be so stuffed I couldn't get around quick in the boat!"

Bruce Canning brought a plate over to join them. "Man-o'-War didn't do badly this morning," he said. "I managed to get a second, and you and Holliger and Fawcett came in fifth, sixth, and seventh. What happened on that first lap, anyhow? I thought you got away right among the leaders."

Luke made no excuses. "Just stupid, I guess," he replied. "We didn't know the course and got becalmed in the lee o' the bluff. If this wind holds we won't make the same mistake this afternoon."

"There were really too many boats starting," said Canning. "Good sailing doesn't count if there are more than twenty or twenty-five in the field. Ought to be a little better in this second race, though. Two sloops were disabled this morning, and I understand a couple more plan to drop out. That should bring it down to thirty or under. Well, good luck to you, boys!"

Luke didn't see Marilyn March at the luncheon, for Mr. Holliger had his party in a private room. But at two-thirty, when they went down to get the *Tern* ready, the girl was there in the group surrounding young Mert. After a moment she slipped away and came over to the dockside.

"Hi," she said. "You did beautifully this morning! Just keep it up!"

Luke introduced her to Axel and the crew man shyly reached up a big hand to shake hers. "It's good to have somebody pullin' for us," he said, grinning. "We'll give it all we've got!"

Then she was gone.

"By golly, boy," murmured Axel admiringly. "She's some girl an' I don't wonder you like her. Too bad her name's on the wrong boat."

Red-faced, Luke kept his attention on the halliard and the peak of the mainsail. "Get the jib up," was all he said.

They cruised out into the open bay and looked around to judge the weather. The wind still held a little west of south and seemed to be fairly steady. There were a few clouds to the northward.

"What do you think?" asked Luke. "Any chance of a thundershower?"

Axel considered the cloud formations. "Not right away, anyhow," he answered. "Maybe not till night. It's comin', though. I've got a prickly feelin' in the back o' my neck— sure sign, my old man says."

The start was at three and they were to sail the same course. Luke had found his tactics good enough in the earlier race, and decided there was no reason to change them, even though the wind was now more southerly. This time they were caught in a snarl of boats near the line and it was only by skillful steering that Luke brought her across among the first dozen. He kept well over toward the east shore on the starboard tack. Pointing high and footing fast, the *Tern* stood ninth or tenth when she came about. And after a short tack to the westward she still held that position when she came over for the beat down to the mark.

Luke glanced back before he made the turn but he couldn't make out any green hull in the pack astern.

"What happened to Holliger?" he asked.

"I thought you saw," said Axel. "The lucky stiff got over the line ahead of everybody. That's him leading now."

Sure enough, through the huddle of sails on the westward leg, Luke caught a glimpse of new white canvas. Grimly he tried to estimate the *Marilyn's* lead. Fifteen lengths? Twenty? Whatever it was, it was too much.

"Ready to come about!" he barked, and whipped the sloop around the buoy.

The wind chose that moment to turn fluky. Hardly were the sails drawing well on the port tack when a flaw shook the jib.

"It's comin' right out o' the west!" Axel called. "Want to go about?"

"No," said Luke. "Maybe it won't last."

He let the Comet fall off to starboard and continued on the same tack, pointing up to the northwest. Ahead of him most of the other boats had tacked. They appeared to be pulling away a little, but ten seconds later his hunch proved right. With temperamental suddenness the wind backed southerly again, blowing in stronger gusts. Luke put the helm down. He could just about make the west mark now. And off to port he could see that at least three of his rivals had been caught aback by the shift. They hung in irons, their headway practically stopped. Before they got squared away the *Tern* was past them.

"Only six ahead of us now!" Axel cried. "We gained on all of 'em, too. By golly, Luke, I bet we can win this race— or come mighty close!"

Luke merely grunted. He knew he had had a break. If the wind hadn't shifted again his strategy would have looked bad. They made the west buoy without another tack and pulled around it in a spectacular jibe, right in the wake of the six leaders.

The run to the northeast was marred by one or two more flaws in the breeze, but since the leading boats were all before the wind there was no change in position. Luke had never seen a race in which the first flight was so tightly bunched. Seven Comets, all planing along with a good following breeze, all so close that the length of a football field would have covered them!

The throng on the clubhouse dock appreciated it, too. The yelling came down to the skippers and their crews in waves, as one boat after another rounded the mark. Seven boats made the turn in not much more than a minute!

Luke had time for only one quick glance at the first sloop, but he saw that her hull was green. Holliger had kept his lead.

14

The wind was almost due south now, and they had to claw their way directly into it. Long tacks were out of the question. Here, Luke told himself, was where speed in coming about would pay off. Axel knew it too. He crouched low to give as little wind resistance as possible and watched his skipper, waiting for the word.

"Now!" called Luke. Hard down on the helm, a touch on the sheet, and the boom came over smoothly as the *Tern* went about. Her sails snapped taut again without loss of way.

On each tack they gained a little. One boat was passed, then another. With a quarter mile to go to reach the south marker, Luke found himself almost abeam of the *Sally C,* running fourth. Canning was close enough to look him in the eye. He wasn't smiling. This was a race and he was in it to win.

With both sloops on the starboard tack and only fifty feet apart, the older skipper suddenly came about. His intention was plain enough—to force the *Tern* to tack as well. Luke judged the rapidly closing gap between them and set his jaw. The other Comet had dropped back a trifle when she tacked, so that their bows were even. With her boom to port the *Tern* had the right of way and Luke kept her on course.

At the last possible second, Canning brought his sloop into the wind and sheered off. As his opponent drove past he waved to show there were no hard feelings.

Luke didn't waste any sympathy on his boss. Canning had tried a bluff and he had called it. Now he had three more boats to think about—especially the green Comet that still held the lead. He made the buoy and swung around it, tacking at once for the westward reach. The number three boat—a trim-looking craft up from Ocean City—was only a couple of lengths ahead.

Just as Luke was planning how he would overtake her the wind lost some of its force and grew puffy. At the same moment a low rumble of thunder reached his ears.

"Oh-oh!" said Axel, peering under the boom. "She's comin', all right—maybe before we can finish."

The black cloud bank that loomed in the northwest told its own story. At home, Luke would have guessed that the storm was half an hour away. Here, he couldn't tell. All he could do was make the best of such wind as still blew, and be ready when it shifted.

Luckily the puffy breeze favored no boat in particular. They all moved jerkily, heeled over one minute and nearly becalmed the next. The ominous sound of thunder continued.

"All I hope," said Luke tensely, "is that we're around the mark and headed south again before those gusts from the north hit us."

Little by little they were hauling up on the third-place sloop. It wasn't brilliant sailing that did it—probably just the fact that the *Tern* had a smoother underside and slipped along more easily. They passed her twenty yards from the buoy. Ahead, the *Marilyn* had just rounded the mark, and the second boat was a bare length behind her. At the same moment Luke caught a fairly strong puff of wind that sent the sloop forward and gave her enough impetus to jibe over and make the turn. A sudden thunder clap, louder and nearer than before, shook the hull. And with it the breeze went completely dead.

Luke had been waiting for something like that. He took one look through the window in the sail, saw the edge of darker water sweeping down under the cloud from the northwest, and put the helm hard over while he still had steerage way.

Ten seconds later, when the first gust hit them, the *Tern* was headed squarely into it. She shivered under the shock but the stays held.

"Hike!" Luke yelled. "Here we go!"

He let her fall off as they shifted sides. The sails filled to the strong wind and the sloop lay over, picking up speed. Roaring along on the port tack, the boys had a moment to take stock of their opponents.

Just ahead of them the number two Comet had blown out her jib and lay head to wind while the crew struggled to free the flapping sail from the shrouds. Astern, Bruce Canning had been caught just as he started to round the marker. Now he was tacking, trying to fetch the buoy again. And where was the *Marilyn*?

"Look!" Axel shouted through the scream of wind. "Holliger's capsized!"

As they scudded past they caught a glimpse of the green hull on its side, and two bedraggled figures in the water, clinging to the edge of the cockpit.

"They're okay—just wet, that's all," Axel called. "We've got this race in our pocket!"

Luke didn't answer. He knew there was no rule compelling him to stop and help a rival in trouble, but he came about just the same. It took two or three minutes to tack back to the overturned sloop.

"Go on—beat it!" Mert Holliger yelled through chattering teeth. "Coast Guard's comin', anyhow."

They heard the roar of a powerful motor as a gray speed launch surged up alongside. Without further delay Luke brought the *Tern* into the wind and got back on course again. It was none too soon. The *Sally C* had rounded the buoy and was coming like a whirlwind.

About that time the wind veered into the west, as Luke had been sure it would. The whole sky was dark now and suddenly the rain came driving down on them. Wet and shivering, the boys raced Canning up the bay, and for two miles the Comets were never more than a length apart.

In the downpour the clubhouse dock looked all but deserted. Then, as they neared the finish line, a few hardy souls came out to watch. What they saw was one of the tightest—and dampest—finishes on record. The *Tern*, in the windward berth, caught a lucky gust as the wind swung southwestward. For a moment the *Sally C* was blanketed and lost the scant yard that would have given her victory. The judges, with their eyes glued to the line, ruled that Luke had crossed first by inches.

*   *   *

The rain stopped shortly after, and by five o'clock the sun was bright and hot. Luke and Axel found a place on the Yacht Club grounds where they could spread out their sails to dry. It was while they were straightening the luff and leech of the mainsail that Bruce Canning came over to congratulate them.

"That was a mighty chivalrous gesture you made," he told Luke with a grin, "but it came close to costing you the race. I suppose I might have done the same thing, only I saw the Coast Guard boat coming. She'd started down the bay as soon as the storm came up."

"I hear some other boats got in trouble," said Luke. "It came up so quick I don't wonder."

"That's right. Four capsized and one lost her topmast.

That cuts down on the points we scored, but our club still did well. We'd have made a real clean sweep if young Holliger hadn't turned over."

Luke half expected Mert to come around and thank him, but the heir to the trucking fortune didn't show up. He must have gone somewhere for a change of clothes after his dunking. What Luke really hoped for was a word from Marilyn. He felt let down when he saw her in the distance aboard the Holliger cruiser, headed down the bay.

While the sails were drying, he went with Axel into the clubhouse. The points for the two races were being figured out and posted. Canning, with seconds in both events, had piled up 29 in the morning and 25 in the afternoon, for an impressive total of 54 points. Right behind him was Luke. He had had a fifth for 26 in the first race. Because fewer boats had finished, his winning afternoon score was 26¼—52¼ points in all. Mert Holliger had only 25 for the day.

It was sunset by the time Luke and Axel had everything secured on the trailer. They drove home without hurry, talking about future races as they went. The Man-o'-War fleet would be sailing most weekends through July and August, with a couple of regattas at other clubs thrown in. Finally, over Labor Day, the race for the Commodore's Cup would be held. That was the event every Man-o'-War skipper pointed for. Other boats were usually invited, but only the home fleet competed for the Cup itself. The winner had his name engraved on the handsome trophy that formed the centerpiece of the Yacht Club showcase.

"Point scores for the season are fine," said Luke. "They get your name in the paper and maybe a shot at the regional championships. But the Cup is what I'd like most to win."

Axel understood him, as any boy raised on the island would.

"Okay," he said, "why not? With all summer to improve, we can give it one heck of a try anyway."

Back at work next morning, Luke was surprised at the number of people who had read of his victory or heard about it by word of mouth. He was kidded a little about beating the boss. Canning went along with the joke and made the comment that if Luke did it again he'd be looking for another job. But actually the boy knew his employer was proud of him. It didn't hurt the firm a bit to have their two names posted at the top of the point scores at the club.

At home, his father and mother took his sailing achievements without any great excitement. They were pleased, of course, but not hysterical, and his sister Joan saw to it that he didn't get a swelled head.

All that month the real estate business continued brisk. Sometimes Luke had to work Saturday afternoons and even Sundays, but he and Axel got into a majority of the local races and continued to place high. Meanwhile Canning had raised his pay and was giving him a larger share of commissions on rentals he made. If his bank account kept on growing he would be sure of enough for his first year of college.

Once or twice a week he took Marilyn out for an evening sail. She had good boat sense to start with and she learned fast. If he had any romantic ideas about the girl he kept them to himself. On her part she seemed content just to sail with him.

Then, early in August, she came to see him at the office one morning. He was busy with a young couple who wanted to look at a list of cottages for sale, and the girl waited. She sat in a corner in her swim suit and beach jacket, slim brown legs crossed, blond hair bent above a travel magazine. Luke left his prospects for a moment, as soon as he could do so politely.

"Hi!" Marilyn smiled. "Guess what—Daddy and

Mother want to get to know you better. Could you come to dinner tomorrow night?"

There was no use trying to conceal his delight. "You know darn well I can," he told her, grinning. "What's more, I will."

"It's a date, then. About seven?" She stood up. "Too bad you can't be on the beach this morning. The surf's extra nice—and nobody to play with but those handsome life-guards!"

"You're making it tough," he said reproachfully. "But I'm afraid duty comes first. See you tomorrow."

Inspired by the Marches' invitation, Luke's salesmanship must have been given a special edge. He got a down payment on a medium-priced bungalow and watched Bruce Canning sign the papers with considerable pride. It was the second sale of a property he had made.

Luke dressed with some care the next evening. The occasion, he thought, called for something more than his usual sport shirt. He put on a white one, with a diagonal-striped bow tie, and wore a white Palm Beach jacket with dark slacks and white buck shoes.

He had had to tell his family why he wouldn't be home for dinner. Joan, inclined to rib him at first, whistled her approval when he came downstairs.

"Wow!" she observed. "Some he-doll! How are you getting down there? Dad's using the Buick. He has to go to Building-and-Loan meeting."

Luke was taken aback. He had forgotten to ask for the car. Oh, well, he thought—he wasn't ashamed to appear on a bicycle.

It was four miles to Crow's-Nest Point and he set off at six-thirty, pedaling along the side of the road with traffic swishing past him. A couple of minutes before seven he entered the driveway, parked his bike, and climbed the steps. Marilyn came to let him in.

Mr. and Mrs. March were sitting at the end of the veranda, looking out over the dunes and the sea. They greeted him warmly.

"I hear you're quite a sailor," said Marilyn's father. He was a trimly built man of forty-five, his brown hair beginning to thin on top. Luke liked his smile.

"Just a beginner," he replied. "So far I've had more than my share of luck."

They went on talking about boats until the boy was completely at ease. Then the maid, Frieda, appeared and announced dinner. At the table, Mrs. March took over the conversation. She was more interested in Luke's ambitions than in his sailing, and under the influence of her smile he was glad to talk.

"I'd like to live here," he said. "Most boys on the island go off to the city and hardly ever come back. But I believe there's a good life down here. Not just in the summer—that's fine, of course—but all year round. You ought to see the ducks and geese and brant that come late in the fall! And the winters are generally mild. We get beautiful days down here when the marshes are all brown and gold and the sea as blue as the sky."

He stopped in some embarrassment. Marilyn was looking at him almost adoringly. Her mother beamed. "You sound like a poet," she said.

"Fine," Mr. March agreed. "But let's hear more about the duck hunting."

That was easy. Luke told them about Bunkie and his exploits—about frosty mornings on the marsh with the decoys.

"Seems to me," he said, "I'd be losing a lot if I went off to work in New York or Philadelphia. That's why I'm so tickled to be with Bruce Canning. He makes a good living here and I'd like to learn all I can about real estate. With a Business Administration course at college, I'm aiming at the same kind of career he has."

"Son," said Mr. March with some feeling, "I hope you

stick to it. Maybe you'll never make a million dollars, but you'll have enough—and a good life, too. I sort of wish I had your chance."

Coming from a vice-president of the Holliger trucking empire, those words took the boy by surprise. He looked down at his plate and finished his dessert.

After their coffee they went back to the veranda. Marilyn turned on the record-player and all four of them danced a while. Mrs. March, herself an excellent dancer, complimented Luke on his easy rhythm when they were partners. All in all it was one of the pleasantest evenings he could remember.

Luke left about ten, explaining that he had to be on the job early next morning. He got on his bicycle and rode down the drive. As he turned into the highway he caught a glimpse of the dark bulk of a car, parked without lights, in the shadow of the high hedge. Neckers, he decided, and thought no more about it.

The night spots in Foremast Harbor were still in full swing and he pedaled carefully through traffic under the bright lights. Then he was out on the lonely road again, his little headlamp throwing a dim beam ten feet or so ahead. A few cars zoomed past and he kept well over on the gravel shoulder. When he was about a mile from home he became aware of headlights behind him, moving only a little faster than he was. He pulled over still farther, to the outer edge of the shoulder, as the car drew abreast.

It was a Cadillac convertible, rolling silently along at eight or ten miles an hour. To Luke's annoyance the side of the car was only a foot from his shoulder and it eased over gradually, pushing him right off into the loose sand.

"Hey!" he shouted as his wheels came to a floundering stop. "What's the idea?"

The only answer was a humorless laugh from the driver of the convertible, now halted beside him.

15

Mert Holliger was alone in the car. He slid into the right-hand seat, vaulted over the door and stood chin to chin with Luke. There was an ugly grin on his face.

"All right," he growled, flexing his big shoulders, "you've been askin' for it, wise guy. Nobody's goin' to steal *my* girl an' get away with it!"

Luke gave the bicycle a push and it fell away from him into the sand. He felt his anger cold and hard inside him.

"Your girl?" he said softly. "Maybe she's the one to decide that."

"I saw you down there tonight," Holliger stormed. "She broke a date for the movies with me. An' you've been takin' her out in your beat-up boat. Stand up now, unless you're scared. I'm goin' to fix you so you'll stay away from her!"

With the words he swung a fist that cut Luke's cheek as he side-stepped. Luke hadn't had a real fight since he was in grade school, but he knew he was in for one now. Twenty pounds lighter than the other boy, he was faster and more wiry. Coolly he jumped to the right, past the car's front fender. The light was better there and he had more room. The bigger youth followed close, cocking his right for another swing, and this time Luke didn't back away. He moved inside, driving his left in a clean jab to his adversary's nose.

Holliger staggered back. There was a look of dazed surprise on his face and his arms were down. Luke could have hit him then while he was helpless, and possibly ended the battle. Instead he waited for another charge.

It came soon enough, but this time Holliger was more cautious. He advanced with his guard high, throwing a left hook toward Luke's jaw. Luke ducked, braced his feet, and slammed his right fist as hard as he could into Holliger's well-fed middle. The gasping grunt he gave was evidence it had hurt. Again his hands dropped, and again Luke had a wide-open chance at that blood-smeared face. Afterward he was glad he didn't take it.

A siren wailed, brakes squealed, and a black-and-white state police car slammed to a stop.

"What goes on here?" the officer demanded gruffly. Luke knew him by sight. His name was Jim Robey and he came from the Marshtown Station.

"We had a—a difference of opinion," Luke stammered. "Came out here to settle it."

"Well, break it up and go on home, both of you. Whose car is this?"

"Mine," said Mert, through puffed lips. "My father's, anyhow. He's Merton Holliger, an' he carries some weight around here."

The implied threat was of no interest to the patrolman. "Let's see your driver's license," he ordered crisply. He took it around into the glare from the Cadillac's headlights to examine it, and it was then that he noticed the bicycle.

"Wait a minute," he said, with a cold eye on young Holliger. "What happened here? Did you run this bike off the road?"

144

"No," Luke put in hastily. "He just drove up alongside slow, so I had to stop. There wasn't any accident."

The officer grinned as he handed back the license. "Maybe you'd better say there *was* one," he remarked. "When you try to explain how you both look to your parents, that is."

He waited till Luke had remounted and started pedaling north, then saw to it that Holliger turned his car around and left in the opposite direction.

Luke could feel a warm trickle down the side of his face, and he knew his white jacket was bloody and torn. When he remembered the look of hurt astonishment in Mert's eyes and the pulpy redness of his nose, he was ashamed. The fight, such as it was, had probably settled nothing. And yet he felt somehow relieved, as if a long-built-up tension had been broken.

Luckily his family had all retired when he stole into the house. He washed off the cut on his cheek-bone and stuck on a bandage, making it as inconspicuous as possible. There was quite a lot of blood spattered on the jacket. He rinsed it out and hung it up to dry before going to bed.

Explanations in the morning were easier than he expected.

"I ran off the road into the sand and got bruised up a bit," he told his mother at breakfast. "Tore my coat, too, but I reckon it can be mended. How about those eggs? Are they ready yet? I don't want to be late for work."

She accepted his white lie without any further questioning. The fact that he was hungry was reassurance enough for her. And his young sister, fortunately, was still in bed, so he didn't have her sharp eyes to contend with.

There was some good-natured kidding at the office—questions like "How's the other guy look?" and "Ran into the bed-post, eh?" But he laughed them off and did his work as usual.

At noon, in the drugstore soda fountain, he saw Johnny Grasso, who missed very little that went on in town. Luke kept the bandaged cheek turned away from him but it was hardly necessary, for Johnny was too full of news to notice.

"Looks like Mert Holliger's finally got what was comin' to him," he said, with a chuckle. "I saw him goin' into the doctor's office an' his face was sure a mess! A shiner on one eye an' a busted nose, among other things. The way I heard it on the grapevine he must ha' gone up to Mizzen Inlet last night an' crashed a Norwegian fishermen's party. Prob'ly gave 'em some lip. So a couple o' those big guys took him outside an' gave him a real goin' over. That ought to teach him."

Luke was satisfied to leave it so. The story reflected little glory on Mert but it might be less damaging to his pride than the truth. Also less likely to reach Marilyn's ears. Luke didn't want the March family to think of him as a brawler.

The cut on his face had practically healed three days later, and he called Marilyn about sailing again. She sounded as glad to be invited as ever. When they were out on the bay she noticed the scar and asked him about it, but accepted his mumbled reply that he had cut himself shaving.

"You know," she told him, "you made a tremendous hit at our house. Dad's been talking about bringing his gun down here next fall and having you and Bunkie take him out after ducks. And Mother liked your manners. 'Now *there*,' she said, 'is a well-brought-up boy.'"

Luke reddened, more pleased than he liked to show. "I'd sure be happy to take your father out on the marsh," he said. "Of course I'll be in college, but I could get down here over weekends and at Thanksgiving. By the way"—

he changed the subject—"would you go to the Yacht Club dance with me Saturday night?"

It was a bold request, and one he had been afraid to make earlier. He wouldn't be surprised at a turn-down.

"Well!" she said, laughing. "It's about time you asked me! I'm happy to accept, Mr. Cramer, and I'll be expecting you at nine o'clock."

❋   ❋   ❋

There was a Comet race that Saturday afternoon, and Luke and Axel came in fifth, after being fouled up at the start. Mert Holliger, for some unannounced reason, wasn't in it. Some thought he wasn't well; others that he was waiting for a new suit of sails.

The season was well along now, and the point scores were piling up. On the clubhouse board Marley Evans still stood first, with 125½. Right behind him were Bruce Canning, with 122¼, and Luke, who had 120¼. Holliger's *Marilyn* had missed some of the racing but still had a respectable 87, for fifth place.

Luke had borrowed the Buick that night and he called for Marilyn promptly at nine. His white jacket, mended, cleaned, and pressed, looked as good as new. Marilyn wore a simple white dance dress that set off her smooth, tanned skin and bright hair. Beyond any question, the boy thought, she was the prettiest girl at the club.

About ten, when the dance was in full swing, he saw Mert Holliger come in with an attractive young brunette. His face showed very little damage, and he seemed to be having a good time. After a while he came strolling toward them.

"Hi, Cramer," he said familiarly, "mind if I cut in?"

Luke watched them dance away with mixed emotions. They certainly made a good-looking couple. But he no longer felt any jealousy. Something told him Marilyn preferred his company.

He danced with a few other girls, happy to see that Marilyn was constantly changing partners. When he came back to her she smiled gratefully.

"Hot, isn't it?" she said. "Let's go out on the deck."

They found a place to sit by the rail, where the moon shone on the quiet water.

"Just in case you were wondering," she told him, "Mr. Holliger, Junior, is no longer one of my close friends. Mother says a fellow who gets his nose broken in a fight is no fit companion for her daughter."

Luke groaned inwardly. It didn't seem fair to Mert to let it go at that. "Marilyn," he said huskily, "maybe you shouldn't be out with me, either. You see—I broke his nose. I didn't mean to, really, but he swung at me and—and—" His voice trailed off.

She squeezed his arm and looked up at him eagerly. "When?" she asked. "When was it?"

"The other night, after I left your house. He'd been waiting. Said he had a movie date with you."

"Well, he didn't," she replied, tossing her head. "I told him we were having a guest to dinner, so I couldn't go. I don't like to have boys fighting over me, but I don't see how it was your fault. There wasn't much else you could do."

Luke drew a deep breath. "Okay," he said. "I'm glad I told you, anyhow. And don't blame Mert too much. This thing had been coming on for a long time."

The evening passed quickly after that, and he got her back to Crow's-Nest within a quarter of an hour of the promised time. At the door she suddenly stood on tiptoe and kissed the scar on his cheek.

"I guessed where you got that before you told me," she

149

laughed. "Don't run into any more swinging doors!" And she ran inside before he could reply.

On the drive home he thought about Mert Holliger's new attitude. Apparently the boy held no grudge, and that hardly seemed like him. Was it possible he had misjudged him after all? Luke was perfectly willing to let bygones be bygones. He decided the best thing to do was accept the apparent armistice but keep himself prepared for a change if it came.

Sunday it rained intermittently, clearing about sunset. Because he had had only five or six hours' sleep the night before, Luke turned in early that evening. It was some time after midnight when he woke to a sound of furious barking. Bunkie was usually a quiet dog and the boy knew something must be wrong. He pulled on a pair of old slacks, grabbed a flashlight, and hurried downstairs.

The black retriever slept outdoors, fastened by a long chain to the corner of the garage. The moment Luke unsnapped it from his collar Bunkie was off, tearing down toward the boat landing on the bay side of the highway. Barefooted, his master raced after him.

When he was still two hundred yards away Luke saw car lights go on and heard the grinding of a starter. The engine roared and the car picked up speed, throwing sand from the rear wheels. Then it was out on the main road, headed south. Bunkie stopped barking and trotted back to Luke's side, a rumbling growl still in his throat.

The boy kept on running. It was close to the *Tern's* trailer that the car had been parked. Breathless, he ran the beam of the light over the boat's hull and up and down the mast and the standing rigging. Nothing seemed to be amiss. He was about to turn back when Bunkie went to the rear of the trailer and barked again.

Luke knelt by the boat's stern, looking underneath. There, hidden by the overhang, was a bunch of rags stuffed between the hull and the crossbar of the trailer. When he reached in and pulled them out, a strong odor came to his nostrils. The rags were soaked in gasoline!

Luke shivered and pulled the big Labrador to him. "Boy," he whispered, "you were just in time. Another minute an' we wouldn't have had a boat!"

16

Before breakfast next morning he went back to the landing to have another look by daylight. Bunkie had been left unchained the rest of the night to prevent a return of the would-be vandals. Now Luke wanted to see if they had left any clues behind. He had his own ideas, of course, but they would be hard to prove.

Search as he would he could discover no evidence near the Comet. Even the tire tracks had been obliterated in the loose sand. He was on his way up toward the highway again when his eye fell on a bit of bright paper close to the sandy track. It was a match cover—not an empty one, but nearly full. On it was the picture of a scantily clad dancing girl and the name of a New York night club. It wasn't much to go on, but he slipped it into his pocket.

As a precaution against further trouble, Luke drove the Buick down, hitched on the trailer, and towed the boat up to the house before he went to work.

He decided to say nothing about what had happened. However, that noon he looked up his friend Johnny Grasso.

"Johnny," he told him, "I want you to help me find out something. Ever hear of a hot spot in New York called the Club Belize? I didn't think you had. I doubt if it's one o' the big ones."

"What's up?" Johnny asked, full of curiosity. "You plannin' to go there?"

Luke laughed. "Not me! But I'd sure like to find out who around here does. You generally hear everything. It could be Holliger or some of his crowd. Why don't you wait for a good chance an' mention the name o' the club? Then see if anybody takes the bait."

"Gee!" said Johnny, his eyes alight. "Real detective stuff, huh? Aren't you goin' to tell me why it's important?"

"Not yet." Luke shook his head. "It probably doesn't mean a thing. I'd just like to know, that's all."

He almost showed Johnny the matchbook cover, then thought better of it. "Remember the name," he said. "Club Belize, on 52nd Street."

Keeping the *Tern* up at the house made things awkward in one way. Luke had to give up his evening sailing with Marilyn. His father was generally using the car, and it was more than a one-man job to push the trailer to the landing by hand.

When he called Marilyn he had to explain that the boat was hauled up. The reason he gave was that he had to do some work on the bottom finish, and he actually did polish it a little, though it had stood up well through the summer.

The last big invitational regatta for the South Jersey region was the third weekend in August. Stone Harbor was the host club. To keep the starting field from being too unwieldy, it was suggested that entries be limited to the top five Comets from each fleet.

With the summer renting season practically over, Bruce Canning was able to give Luke all day Saturday, and take the same time off himself. Once again the boat trailers took to the Garden State Parkway, this time headed south. It was a fine, cool morning as Luke and Axel drove down the big road between pines and marsh.

They reached the Stone Harbor exit before nine-thirty and drove at once to the Yacht Club. An impressive array of boats already filled the trailer parking space and others were in the water. Flags were flying. The whole place had an air of bustle and festivity. Stone Harbor bore the proud title of Comet Fleet No. 1, and among its members were two past national champions.

After registering, the two boys got the *Tern* into the basin. It was a quick and easy job, with an electric hoist to speed things up. As soon as their sails were set they cruised out of the basin to test the course and the wind.

The morning race would be sailed in the main channel, with a dog-leg westward into Great Sound. Since a fairly brisk southeasterly breeze was blowing, they would be before the wind at the start, finishing the lap with a beat back to the line. The tide was nearing flood but still running up-channel.

Ten minutes before the eleven o'clock start, twenty-seven Comets were maneuvering in the bay. Most of them were making short tacks south of the starting line, but a few chose to go up the channel, counting on getting back before the start. One of them, Luke saw, was last year's national Comet champ, Dane Miller, in a tan-painted boat called the *Zipalong*.

"He ought to know what he's doing," Luke speculated aloud. And boldly he followed the Stone Harbor skipper's wake.

"Watch your time," Axel warned him. "There goes the blue."

The tan boat came about fast, heading for the outer line marker on the port tack. At once Luke put his own sloop into the wind. He was a few yards to leeward and two lengths astern. With a minute to go they were close to the starting line but facing what looked like an impenetrable blanket of other sails. Miller had enough headway to slide safely over, bring his boat about and make a beautiful start, right with the gun. The *Tern* wasn't quite as lucky. Caught by a crowd of other boats when he was halfway across the line, Luke had to let her drift another three or four yards before he could put her helm down. And by the time she filled away before the wind two-thirds of the fleet had gone over ahead of her.

"I guess," said Luke ruefully, "you have to be a real champion to get your timing just right on a stunt like that."

They settled down to sailing, running wing-and-wing before the following breeze. It wasn't easy to overtake the boats ahead, for today they were competing against the pick of the fleets. Some fifteen Comets still led the *Tern* when she rounded the north buoy and headed westward.

Luke was glad to hold his own on that broad reach into Great Sound. He knew his best chance would come later, when they started beating back.

"I can see Holliger up ahead," Axel announced. "He must ha' got a pretty good start. He's runnin' about fourth or fifth, right ahead o' the *Sally C*."

Luke kept out to windward, knowing a break-through to the lee was practically impossible on a reach. Shortly before the end of the westward leg he was able to blanket the boat just ahead and to leeward and pulled out better than a length in front. The turn had to be made from the port side of the mark. That called for a jibe, and they executed it perfectly, coming up inside the next Comet and passing her within a hundred yards.

Again the *Tern* was demonstrating her speed on the wind. They made a close reach of it back to the north buoy and disposed of still another rival on the way. That left a round dozen sloops ahead, and Luke could see that so far they were gaining very little on the leaders.

He kept his body low to cut down drag and nursed

the boat along with a light hand on the tiller. She was pointing beautifully—closer to the wind, he thought, than almost any other Comet in the race. He measured the length of his tacks with care. Twice their speed in coming about saved them distance and dropped fresh rivals astern. They were at the heels of the first flight when they passed the clubhouse.

The lower buoy was a few hundred yards south, just above the drawbridge. It would require a full 180-degree turn, and Luke was making his approach on the starboard tack when the leading boats came past before the wind. He saw Miller's tan sloop on top, followed by Marley Evans's *Gull*. Next was a sloop from the Sea Isle City club, with Bruce Canning pushing him hard. And the *Marilyn* was in a neck-and-neck battle with another Stone Harbor boat for fifth position.

As they passed each other on opposite courses Luke couldn't see Holliger's face, but for a second he had a good look at Lonny Sholtz. The crew man was a stocky youngster with a swept-back mane of black hair that started close to his eyebrows. He recognized the *Tern* and his sullen, pouty face twisted in a grin that was almost a sneer. He yelled something but it was carried off by the wind.

Luke fetched the mark, rounded it from the port side, jibed and let the sheet run. For the moment the *Tern* was pretty much by herself in tenth place. The ninth boat was leading her by three lengths and the eleventh was about the same distance astern. Axel had raised the centerboard and edged aft for the run north.

"Who's that gorilla crewin' for Mert?" he asked.

"Name's Sholtz," Luke told him. "I hear he's a friend—goes to the same military school."

"Well," the Norwegian boy replied, "he doesn't look

156

very military to me. Or friendly, either. I can stand his skipper sometimes but that guy's a real creep!"

The wind was steady but not quite strong enough to get the boat planing. The ten leading Comets went up the bay with no visible change in their positions. Luke thought he had reduced the distance between the *Tern* and the next boat ahead, but it was hard to be sure.

Now that the tide was past flood they would have no current to help them until the return trip. When they rounded the north marker and headed west, the race began to tighten up. Luke succeeded in passing one opponent on the reach. He was right behind another when they made the turn. And on the close reach to the east, two more rivals were overtaken. They had moved up into seventh place, with the *Marilyn* almost within hailing distance.

Mert Holliger must have seen who was following him. The *Tern* was coming up on his weather quarter, and just before they reached the north buoy he luffed to force Luke out of position. The strategy worked temporarily. Unable to cut inside, Luke fell astern and rounded in the green boat's wake.

They were on the last leg of the race now. A mile and a half against a head wind would tell the story. Luke believed he could outpoint Holliger. He deliberately chose the opposite tack from the green sloop and headed for the eastern shore of the bay, sails flat and heeled well over. Holliger appeared to be pulling away but he would have to come about before long. The moment he did, Luke put his own helm down and swung over on the port tack.

He looked up at the wind vane and ahead at the distant finish line. There was a chance, he thought, that they could make it on this one tack. At least they could come close.

"Get down an' keep your fingers crossed," he told Axel. "I'm going to point as high as she'll take it."

He crouched low along the windward side and fingered his sheet and tiller gently, keeping the sloop's nose pointing just inside the outer mark, yet trying not to lose speed. The ebbing tide helped. True, the current caused some choppiness, but there was little side slip.

"Here comes Mert," Axel called out. "An' by golly we've got him!"

Like the *Tern*, the *Marilyn* was on the port tack now. It looked as if she might be moving faster through the water, but she wasn't as close to the wind. A minute later she crossed astern of them, hauling out to leeward.

The leaders, too, were drawing closer as they made short tacks, getting into position for the line. Miller's *Zipalong* and Evans's *Gull* still ran one-two, and both were well to windward, sure of finishing on the port tack. Bruce Canning had passed the Sea Isle boat but he was now too far to leeward, off to starboard of the *Tern*. As the boys watched he came about, scudding across their bows without stealing their wind.

Luke held his course. As the finish line approached and the shouts of the spectators came to them down the wind, he knew his boat would make it. With only a foot or two to spare he ran inside the outer mark, beating the *Sally C* by half a length. The *Marilyn* came in fifth.

The Stone Harbor skippers were famous for their hospitality, and they fairly outdid themselves on this occasion. A huge lunch was served the visitors, and some of the older sailors refreshed themselves at the bar.

Axel took a look at the highballs being lifted and nudged Luke's arm. "There's a few guys we won't have to worry about this afternoon," he said, chuckling. "They'll be lucky not to ram each other."

"Or us," said Luke, with a frown. "We'd better keep clear of 'em."

159

Marilyn March was waiting on the basin dock when they went back to the boat. Her eyes were sparkling.

"You two old salts made quite a name for yourselves," she told them. "Seventeenth getting over the line and came in third! Once you learn something about starts, Luke, you'll be pretty good."

He grinned and hung his head. "How'll I learn if I don't take chances?" he asked. "Anyhow, we'll try being conservative this afternoon and see how we do."

"I'll be watching," she said. "It's going to be sailed over in Great Sound, but Mr. Holliger's taking Dad and me out there in his cruiser."

Great Sound was a fairly large body of open water, three or four miles across. The course was a triangle: first west, then northeast, then southeast. Luke had a chart that showed it. A few shoals were marked, and a deep-water channel which was part of the coastal inland waterway.

They took the *Tern* out early and sailed into the sound to scout the course.

"See those channel stakes?" Luke remarked. "We've got to watch 'em. With the tide going out, and in strange water, we don't want to run aground anywhere."

Other boats were soon clustering about the starting line. It was between two anchored cruisers, occupied by members of the Race Committee. When they hoisted the white flag, Luke checked his watch. With the wind still south-by-east, he figured his best plan would be to get well to the northward and come down on the port tack, ready to cut across at the final signal.

Quite a few other skippers seemed to have the same strategy, though Luke noticed that Miller was off to the southward, preparing to run up to the start before the wind.

At the blue flag Luke came about. He had figured the distance back to the line carefully and he knew just about how fast the *Tern* would move on this slant. The only difficulty might come from the jam of other sloops on the same course.

With a minute to go he succeeded in slipping through between two opponents into the front rank of jockeying boats. He passed the upper end of the starting line just as the *Zipalong*, running free, came bowling up from the south. Both boats had their booms to starboard, and the right of way belonged to the *Tern*—the sloop sailing close-hauled. They passed each other right at the middle of the line. And at that second the red flag was hoisted.

Luke had been as close to the line as he dared. Now, as he let the bow fall off, he was neck-and-neck with Miller and a little to windward, fighting for the lead.

"Nice goin', boy!" Axel cheered. "I hope your girl friend was watchin' *that* start!"

17

The tan-painted Comet was fast, as Luke soon discovered. And she was beautifully handled. In spite of the advantage of his own windward position, his efforts to blanket her were all in vain. Miller kept her just out of reach and pulled ahead inch by inch. At the end of the westward reach the *Tern* trailed by three-quarters of a length, and Luke had to let the *Zipalong* jibe around the buoy first.

Bruce Canning had made a good start, too. No sooner had Luke made the turn than he found the *Sally C* a length behind him and to windward. They were on a broad reach to the northeast and there was nothing safe about a leeward berth. If Canning gained a little, as he seemed to be doing, there was real danger of being blanketed.

There was only one thing Luke could do. He fell off to port, widening the distance between their courses and getting away from the other sloop's blanketing cone. It dropped him to third place for the moment, but he hoped to make it up on the southward beat.

Across the angle of the course they could see the rest of the field, most of them still reaching west on the first leg. Suddenly one sloop broke away from the others and came careering northward before the wind.

"Hey!" yelled Axel. "Is that guy crazy? He's way off course!"

They saw the crew man scramble aft and heard loud voices raised in an altercation, but the wandering Comet still rushed toward them. It missed the *Sally C's* stern by inches. If Luke had had more warning he might have come up into the wind, but the runaway sloop was too close for that now. In desperate haste he jerked the helm up, slacked the sheet, and fell off to leeward barely in time. Even as he did so he saw the channel stake abeam. It marked the edge of shoal water. With a shivering jolt that threw both boys into the cockpit, the *Tern* rammed her nose into a mud bank.

Luke was dazed but unhurt. He got to his feet and helped Axel up. The young Norwegian had hit his head on the centerboard well and a cut over his eye was bleeding. They were too disgusted to say a word as Luke tied a handkerchief around Axel's forehead. Then they got over the side and struggled through the mud to the bow.

Pushing didn't stir the stranded Comet, no matter how hard they tried. As they sweated at the job a jeering laugh came to them on the wind. The *Marilyn* was going by, and Lonny Sholtz was yelling taunts in their direction.

"Okay," said Luke through gritted teeth, "maybe the wind's holding her on. Guess I'll have to lower the main sail."

"Wait," Axel urged. "Give her one more try. We'll lift up more on the bow this time."

They got their hands underneath and strained upward. There was a sucking sound, and reluctantly the boat's bottom came out of the mud. They pushed her free and tumbled aboard. With Axel holding her off the shoal with an oar, Luke trimmed the sheet and sailed her out to windward. Behind them, still fast in the mud, was the sloop that had caused all the trouble.

"Know that fathead of a skipper?" asked Axel with a growl. "He's one o' the boys that was bendin' an elbow at the club. I bet he won't be invited back soon!"

Their mishap had cost them dearly. Every other Comet still afloat was ahead of them now, and the leaders were already nearing the north marker. Worse than that, however, was the scraping the *Tern* had taken. Luke could feel the drag on the bottom. The mud that must be sticking to the centerboard would wash away in time. The real trouble was that the sloop's skin was no longer smooth. She struggled gallantly after the rest of the fleet, but in his heart Luke knew it was hopeless.

Axel could sense her sluggishness, too. "Any chance o' catchin' up?" he asked glumly.

Luke shook his head. "We won't quit, though," he said. "Somebody else could have tough luck, too, an' we might pick up a point or two."

They finally reached the turn and started the beat southward. Always fastest when she was close-hauled, the *Tern* picked up a little. She came about as handily as ever, and soon she was passing slower boats. Three of them were astern when they rounded the south buoy. But on the reach to the west she barely held her own, and her performance was no better on the second leg.

A Coast Guard launch had come up the sound and pulled the drunk off the shoal. They could see his Comet being towed home as they passed the spot.

Gaining a little, as she had before on the final leg, the *Tern* succeeded in passing one more sloop before she crossed the finish line. It was a pretty sorry showing.

Luke looked up to see Marilyn waving from the foredeck of the Holliger cruiser. He waved back and even managed a sheepish grin. But he was glad she was too far away to ask him questions.

At the clubhouse several skippers he knew came up to

commiserate with him. To his surprise, one of them was the famous Dane Miller. He was a quiet, almost shy young man with a pleasant grin.

"Darn shame that fool had to spoil your race," he said. "You had a swell start, an' I expected to have my hands full with you all the way. I've heard a lot o' sailors say yours'll be the boat to beat next year."

With that kind of encouragement Luke felt a little better. The point scores were being posted on the board, and his third had given him twenty-four points for the morning race. In the afternoon he had scored only a lowly four. Canning and Evans, in the meantime, had piled up better than forty points each, and Mert Holliger had gathered a total of thirty-nine.

The boys hoisted the *Tern* on the trailer and set out for home. One look at her bottom had told Luke he had a lot of work to do before Labor Day. Under the mud that still clung to the planking he had found the paint scratched and rough. There were always broken clamshells and other debris in marsh muck. The force with which the boat had struck the shoal had scraped her underside on many of these sharp edges.

"No wonder the poor old gal was slow," said Axel. "I'll come down tomorrow an' we'll work on her."

The Stone Harbor regatta still had one race to sail on Sunday, but Luke knew he would have no chance with the *Tern* in that condition. The other members of the Man-o'-War club all stayed down there, and the boy reflected with some bitterness that Holliger would probably come home ahead of him in points for the season.

Sunday morning Axel came down from Mizzen Inlet and the boys tackled the job. With all traces of mud removed, the damage to the hull didn't look quite so bad. Two hours of labor with coarse sandpaper got rid of the scratches. Then they applied fine sandpaper to produce the right surface for painting. Luke still had some of the paint he had used back in the spring, and he put on a primer coat that night. When he went to the office Monday morning he was able to report that the *Tern* would be ready to sail on Labor Day.

Bruce Canning was sympathetic. "I thought you had a good chance to win that second race," he said. "You were giving Miller all he wanted. From what I hear, the guy who took a few too many at lunch is going to be thrown out of the Association. It's the first time such a thing has happened in years, and I doubt if you'll ever see anything like it again. Most Comet sailors are a good, clean bunch, and too smart to get in that kind of trouble."

Luke asked him about the point standings and he produced a list of the club's top skippers he had copied from the board. Marley Evans, with a second, a fifth, and a seventh in the three regatta races, had a season total of 188½. Canning himself had finished fourth, sixth, and third, and now had 185¼. Luke came next with 148½, and Mert Holliger, who had come in sixth on Sunday, trailed him closely with 144.

Johnny Grasso was over in the drugstore at lunch-time, down-hearted because he had nothing to report. "Everybody was away over the weekend," he said. "All down at Stone Harbor, I guess. We had mighty little business at the Yacht Club, an' the old fogies who were around didn't any of 'em look as if they'd ever been in a night club. I sure wish you'd tell me why you're interested, though."

Luke hesitated, then brought out the matchbook cover. "All right," he said. "Somebody tried to burn my boat the other night. Whoever it was came in a car. There were rags soaked in gasoline under the hull. I guess they were all ready to light 'em, only my dog was barking and I ran down to the landing with him. Must have scared 'em off. All I could find next morning was this."

Johnny examined the cover, big-eyed with excitement. "A clue, huh? Okay, boss, your private eye is on the job! Just one thing—which way was the car headed when it pulled out?"

"South," said Luke, and the Italian boy nodded.

"I thought so. Looks like they came from down this way. I'll see what I can dig up."

Later that week Luke called up Marilyn and dated her for the movies. He found she had watched the Saturday afternoon race from somewhere near the middle of the triangle, and had had a fair view of his disaster.

"I could see the idiot didn't know where he was going," she said. "And when everybody began yelling at him I thought he'd come back on the course. Then I saw you and it looked as if he might run right into you. I prayed, Luke. I wanted you to win that race."

He laughed. "Well," he told her, "it was partly my own fault. I should have brought her into the wind when I first saw him coming, and it would only have cost me a few lengths. Anyhow, the boat's going to be all right if I can get her painted. Lucky I had these two weeks to work on her. If she's finished in time we can have one good sail before the Commodore's Cup."

He put in two or three hours on the sloop nearly every night. He painted, sanded, and repainted, allowing the coats to dry between-times. Finally, on Friday evening of the last week in August, he ran his hand over the mirror-smooth bottom and decided the *Tern* was as ready as she would ever be.

He heard the phone ringing in the house. A moment later his mother came to the door and called to him. "It's for you, Luke. I think it's Axel Gundersen, and he wants to talk to you."

Axel's voice had a queer, muffled sound. "I'm sort o'

laid up, Luke," he said. "Hate to tell you, but it looks like I can't crew for you Monday."

"Gosh!" Luke groaned in consternation. "Honest? What happened?"

"I went out with one o' the skiffs after school tuna, this mornin'. They were hittin' pretty fast an' I got my wrist fouled in a line an' dragged overboard. By the time they pulled me out my wrist was cut pretty deep an' I was full o' salt water. The doc says I've got to stay in bed or I'll get pneumonia."

"I sure am sorry," Luke told him. "But you quit worrying and get well. Do what the doctor tells you. I'll find a crew somewhere."

He could understand readily enough how the accident had happened. The bank skiffs used heavy hand-lines and trolled with big metal squid for bait. With outriggers, they might have six or eight lines out at once. And when they got into a school of blues or tuna, things were likely to happen fast. A hard-fighting twenty-pounder could jerk a man who was off balance right out of the boat—particularly if his wrist was snagged by a loop of line.

As to his reassuring promise that he would find a crew, he was less optimistic than he sounded. He and Axel had made a fast, smooth-working team, and he couldn't think of anybody else who might fill the Norwegian boy's shoes.

Luke was feeling worried when he rode his bicycle down the island Saturday morning. Johnny Grasso was a possibility. Before going to the office, Luke stopped at the shoe repair shop, hoping to find him. The boy wasn't there but his father said if he saw him he would send him around.

Bruce Canning heard the news and tried to cheer Luke up. However, he was able to offer no promising suggestions. Practically every sailor on the island was either skipper of his own boat or already signed up as crew. Luke had just about resigned himself to waiting for next year when he saw Johnny coming in the door.

Johnny's face was shining. "Hey!" he burst out. "Wait till you hear what I've got to tell you!"

Hastily Luke took him over to a corner of the office where they wouldn't be heard. "I suppose you've found out what I asked you to," he said, "only I'm afraid it won't do me any good now."

"What do you mean—won't do you any good?" asked Johnny, astounded. "Yeah, I found out all right, but that's not the half of it. Listen—they had a fire at Holligers' last night. Mert caught that friend o' his—that Lonny Sholtz—tryin' to get away after it started. He was sore at Mert's father because he wouldn't let him take one o' the cars, so he set out to burn the garage, cars an' all! They put it out in time an' the State Police took Sholtz in. Seems he had a record before—reg'lar firebug! An' get this—when they searched him he had a book o' matches from the Club Belize!"

Luke stood there open-mouthed, trying to take it all in. He didn't wonder that Johnny was excited.

"Well, I'll be darned!" he said. "I'm glad it wasn't Mert that tried to burn my boat. Guess this leaves him in the same fix I'm in—no crew. Axel's laid up and can't sail with me. I came around to the shop this morning to see if you could get off from your job at the club and crew for me."

Johnny's face fell. "Oh, gosh!" he replied unhappily. "I wish I'd known. I signed on to sail with Mert half an hour ago!"

Luke managed a grin. He gave Johnny's shoulder a friendly punch. "Don't worry about it," he said. "You're in a good boat an' I wish you luck. Don't happen to know any other loose crew men, do you?"

Frowning, Johnny shook his head. Then suddenly he

looked up, his eyes brightening. "Yes!" he almost shouted. "I know who you can get, an' a good crew, too! That March girl—she'd give her right arm to sail in a race with you. Have you tried to get her?"

"No," said Luke, reddening. "I don't know why, but somehow I hadn't thought about it. She's a good sailor all right."

"Well, you big dope," Johnny cried, "get on the phone and ask her!"

18

That afternoon Luke rerigged the *Tern* and put her in the water. His father gave him a hand with the mast and by three o'clock she was shipshape once more. He sailed down the bay to pick up his new crew.

Johnny's advice had been sound. There was no doubt about the eagerness in Marilyn's response when he telephoned her. And she was waiting impatiently on the dock when he brought the sloop to land.

Lightly she jumped aboard, picked up the oar, and fended off. Then she took her proper place on the windward side, ready for orders.

"I'm honestly sorry for Axel," she said, "and I know I'm not as good as he is. But oh, Luke, I've wanted this chance so much! I promise I won't let you down."

"You'll do fine," he told her heartily. "And," he added with an approving glance at her costume of shorts and jersey, "if the race was a beauty contest we'd win in a walk."

The wind was light that day but they got in some good practice on tacking, jibing, and sailing before the wind. Marilyn knew what she was supposed to do and did it fast. Except in a really stiff breeze, the fact that she weighed sixty pounds less than Axel might be an advantage rather than a handicap.

As they made a reach of it up past the Yacht Club they saw a green-hulled Comet coming down the channel. Mert Holliger and Johnny Grasso were taking their own practice sail.

"Hi, Cramer," the young skipper called cheerfully, "want to swap crews?"

"Nope," said Luke. "I'm satisfied for now. Tell you better after the race Monday."

"That's right," Holliger replied with a laugh. "And good luck! I'm warning you right now—you're goin' to need it!"

Since the evening before, Man-o'-War Island had begun to hum with activity like a hive of bees. The usual throng of holiday week-enders was still arriving, and every cottage, apartment, and hotel room was filled.

Luke went to church with his family Sunday morning. Afterward he drove north to the Gundersens' house at Mizzen Inlet. Axel was propped up in bed, feeling enough better to joke a little about his mishap. But his wrist was painfully swollen under the bandages and his voice was still hoarse.

"You find a crew yet?" he asked. "I've been lyin' here worryin'."

When Luke told him who was sailing in his place, Axel looked relieved. "That's swell!" he said. "You two ought to do all right."

"I guess you wouldn't have heard," Luke went on, "but Mert Holliger's got a new crew, too—Johnny Grasso. That young thug he had before has gone to jail!"

Axel's eyes fairly popped as he listened to the story. "Holy cow!" he said. "With a guy like that around, you sure were lucky to scare him off before he burned the *Tern*. You get her refinished all right? How's she go?"

"She's as slick as ever. If we don't win tomorrow it'll be my fault, not the boat's."

"Good!" said Axel. "Wish I could be there, but I'll be pullin' hard for you."

* * *

Labor Day morning came in cool, breezy, and sunny. It looked like ideal sailing weather when Luke got up. He hurried through breakfast and went to the landing at once. There was no trace of dew on the *Tern's* paint or standing rigging, but he rubbed it all down with the chamois anyhow. The wind was in the southeast, he saw, strong and steady. The tide was beginning to come in and should be close to full flood by race time.

When he carried the sails down, the whole family came with him. Joan helped him with the slides while he threaded the bolt rope into the boom.

"Where are you going to pick up your crew?" she asked, a little jealous. "Do you have to sail all the way down to her place?"

"She'll probably be at the Yacht Club," Luke replied. "Anyway, I'll stop there and see. It's still plenty early."

But when he looked up a moment later the white Thunderbird was coming down the road to the landing. Marilyn got out and he introduced her to his parents and sister. The older girl was so friendly and unaffected that Luke could sense an immediate mellowing in Joan's attitude.

"I couldn't wait," Marilyn laughed. "If I'm going to be any help to Luke, I need all the practice I can get. Are you are all going to watch the race?"

"Wouldn't miss it!" said Seth Cramer. "I've never been much of a fan before, but Luke's got me sold. Even Mother's getting excited. We'll all be down at the clubhouse when you start."

They got the *Tern* into the water and Luke's father

pulled the trailer up. "Good luck!" he yelled after them as the sails filled.

Luke trimmed the sheet and headed south on a long slant, close-hauled. The breeze was strong and Marilyn lay back, hiked far out to windward.

"Ooh, what a sailing morning!" she exclaimed. "Don't you love it when it's like this?"

"If it stays like this, yes. Wouldn't want that wind to freshen too much, though. I hope you ate a big breakfast, because we'll need the ballast."

They tacked into the Yacht Club basin and tied up. In the clubhouse the skippers had begun to gather. Luke took Marilyn to the Race Committee table and reported his change of crew. Mr. Cobley looked sternly at the girl over his glasses.

"Can't sail without a membership," he huffed at her with his usual lack of tact.

Marilyn smiled sweetly. "Will this do?" she asked, and handed him her Associate Membership card.

"Hmm," he grunted. "Seems to be all right. That your name—March?"

"Yes. I'm George March's daughter," she answered proudly.

"Oh, that's different. Glad to approve you, Miss March."

Over Cobley's shoulder Luke caught a wink of amusement from Marley Evans. The Commodore was standing there in full regalia, brass-buttoned blue coat and all.

"Aren't you sailing today, Mr. Evans?" the boy asked.

"Not today, Luke. I wish I could, but it's a sort of tradition that the Commodore stays out of this race."

"Well, it's a break for the rest of us, I guess. But we'll miss you, sir," said Luke, and meant it.

The chart of the course was on the bulletin board. It was a little longer than usual today, for the start would be southward, into the wind. They had to make a circuit of the south buoy before heading north, then west into Dutchman's Bay and back, twice around.

"Good," Luke whispered to his crew. "That gives me a chance to try a new kind of start. I'll tell you about it later."

By ten-thirty the channel was full of Comets testing their wings. Except for Marley Evans, every skipper in the fleet—more than twenty boats in all—was out for this one. Luke kept well to leeward, out of earshot of any competitor, while he outlined his starting strategy. Marilyn was delighted.

"It sounds wonderful if it's timed just right," she said.

"And if it isn't," Luke answered with a grin, "we'll look like the biggest chumps on the bay. It's worth a try, though, and if you're game we'll take a chance."

He watched the wind anxiously in those last minutes, but there was no sign of its shifting or dying down. It still blew out of the southeast. At the ten-minute signal he set his watch as usual. For the next five minutes they cruised off to the westward with apparent aimlessness. All the other sloops were working back and forth to the north of the line, so densely packed that hardly one of them had sea room. If any of them noticed the *Tern* there was no sign of it.

"There's the blue signal," said Marilyn tensely. "Shall we come about?"

"Not quite yet," Luke answered, trying to sound calm and collected. "All I need is two minutes."

He checked his watch again, then brought the sloop slowly into the wind. She hung there a moment, sails flapping.

"All right," he said at last. "Here we go."

With helm hard down he brought the *Tern* over on the starboard tack. They were some two hundred yards to leeward of the starting line, and only thirty feet or so behind it. The sloop lay over, moving fast, with the wind booming over her starboard bow.

When there was one minute to go, Luke knew he had calculated right. He was headed for a point just north of the leeward marker, while almost all the other skippers in the fleet were jockeying to cross on the port tack. Before their astonished eyes he drove along above the line, blocking their path. And since he had the right of way there was nothing they could do about it.

The only difficulty was that he was coming dangerously close to the windward mark. At the last split second the starting gun sounded.

"Ready about!" he barked and jammed the tiller down. Marilyn ducked swiftly as the boom came over. The sloop's nose missed the mark by a yard. In the same instant she crossed the line, footing fast on the port tack.

"It worked!" gasped Marilyn. "I've been holding my breath for ages but you made it! We've got the lead!"

At least six other sloops had made good starts. Luke saw that he was less than a length ahead of the *Sally C,* and off to leeward of her were others, all neck-and-neck. One of them was Mert Holliger's green Comet, cutting the water with more speed than he had ever seen her show before. Luke trimmed his own sheet with care and the *Tern* heeled still farther, her gunwale skimming through the creaming seas. Yet when he looked again the green boat was even with him, a good length ahead of the rest of the contenders.

Under the tip of the boom Luke had a slanting view of the *Marilyn's* stern. But the name on the transom didn't look like *Marilyn*. He rubbed his eyes and stared once more.

"Hey!" he whooped. "Holliger's changed the name of his boat! Take a look through the window."

The girl, high on the windward gunwale, twisted her body till she could see. "You're right!" she cried. "It's the *Haulfast II*. Do you suppose Mert has finally seen the light?"

"Looks like it," said Luke. "But right now, whatever her name is, we've got to catch her! Get as low as you can, and keep down the wind drag."

Being to windward had one advantage. Holliger would have to point extra high to fetch the south mark without tacking. Luke, on his present course, could make it easily. As they rushed down toward the buoy he saw the sail of the *Haulfast II* flatten, and she began to pull closer. Meanwhile the *Tern* had gained. Her nose crept past the other sloop's and the disturbed wind off her sails threatened to blanket her opponent. Holliger was helpless. He couldn't crowd inside to make the marker and it was too late for him to tack. All he could do was fall off, jibe, and come around to the port side of the buoy again.

While he was doing it Luke rounded the mark, jibed quickly and headed north after the 180-degree turn. He had gained a lead of three good lengths. And when he looked back, Bruce Canning's *Sally C* had also passed the *Haulfast II*.

They had a broad reach now, all the way to the northern mark, two miles up the bay. With her weight no longer needed for ballast, Marilyn slid aft to sit by Luke.

"Mert looked pretty upset," she remarked. "Wasn't there anything he could have done about it?"

"Not after I had an overlap," said Luke. "He couldn't hail me to come about as long as I was in position to fetch the mark on the course I was sailing. That's covered in the International Yacht Racing Rules—number thirty-two, I think. Anyhow, he's a long way from out of it yet. Look at him come!"

The green boat was fastest with the wind abaft her

beam, and Holliger was making the most of this leg. He had caught the *Sally C* and seemed to be gaining a little on the *Tern*. Luke shifted the helm a point to starboard. He didn't want his rival sneaking up in the weather berth where he could steal his wind.

The sun that had been shining on Marilyn's bright hair was suddenly dimmed. Glancing up, Luke saw small, high clouds scudding over from the east.

"Does that mean it's going to rain?" the girl asked.

"No," he told her, "but it could mean a change of wind. We've got to keep an eye peeled for flaws. And if there's a real shift, it may swing to the east."

Halfway between the clubhouse and the north buoy the *Tern* was still ahead, but not by much. Holliger was creeping up on her lee and Canning held on, two or three lengths astern. Four other sloops had pulled away from the pack and were in contention.

"Look," said Marilyn, "is that a flaw coming?"

"Off to starboard Luke saw an edge of dark, ruffled water sweeping across from the eastern shore of the bay.

"Good girl!" he exclaimed, and trimmed the sheet just as the gust of wind hit them. They hooked their feet in the hiking straps and were ready to balance the sudden heel of the boat.

Canning had seen it coming and been prepared, but Mert Holliger was caught napping. The wind fluttered his mainsail before he could haul the sheet and he lost way for a moment.

The breeze steadied. It was right abeam now, and more to the *Tern's* liking. Once again she began to inch away from her pursuers. Marilyn grinned at Luke and drew a deep, ecstatic breath. "We're gaining," she cried. "Nobody'll catch us now!"

"Whoa, there," Luke said, laughing. "An awful lot can happen in a sailing race, and we haven't finished even a quarter of it yet. You'd better get ready to set the whisker pole. We'll be going around that marker in a minute."

Obediently she scrambled forward and took the pole from the cuddy. "I know what I said was silly," she said contritely. "You'll just have to remember I never sailed in a race before."

Abreast of the buoy Luke slacked the sheet and let the bow fall off. With mainsail to port and jib to starboard, the *Tern* started her run before the wind into Dutchman's Bay. Looking behind him, the young skipper saw the *Sally C* round the mark, followed at once by the *Haulfast II*. Several others were close behind.

"Come back here with me," Luke ordered his crew, "and sit up as tall as you can. Maybe we can get her planing."

As it turned out, the wind wasn't quite strong enough, but the sloop held her own. As they passed the entrance to the short-cut through the marsh, Luke looked astern again. He had a hunch Mert Holliger would head for it and he was right. Perhaps he should have used it himself. The tide was still high, and there would be plenty of water, but the cut was so narrow that a sloop running wing-and-wing would certainly brush the marsh grass on either side.

He had to admire Holliger's nerve and skill. With her boom knocking down the reeds, the *Haulfast II* plowed straight through the cut. And when she came out she was a length and a half in front.

"See what I mean?" said Luke. "This race is a long way from over."

19

Mert Holliger's boldness had paid off. He kept his lead right down to the western marker, with the *Tern* and the *Sally C* trailing. But Luke knew the short-cut could only be used in one direction. For the *Tern*, coming back against an east wind, tacking would be impossible in that narrow strip of water.

The *Haulfast II* swung tight around the buoy and Johnny Grasso waved gaily at the sloop that chased her. Luke was too busy to wave back. Gauging the distance, he brought the helm up at the right second and the *Tern* came about with a rush. As soon as she had speed enough, he put her over on the port tack.

"Now," he told Marilyn, "we'll see who's fastest close-hauled."

Holliger had chosen to stay on the starboard tack till he was close to the north bank. Luke, with plenty of sea room, held the opposite slant. He knew his boat would point high, and he figured if he could get far enough to the southeast he might be able to fetch the upper mark with only one more tack.

When the *Haulfast II* came about it was hard to tell which Comet had the lead. Both were beating southeast-ward, both heeled over to the limit. Luke, in the leeward berth, picked his moment and put the helm down for a fast tack. Then, with the wind over his starboard bow, he headed straight for the distant north buoy. Through the plastic window in the mainsail he could see his rival coming swiftly on what looked like a collision course.

Marilyn was leaning far out to windward, and the boom hid the approach of the green-hulled sloop from her. Perhaps, Luke thought, it was just as well. They were heading for what seemed to be a certain crash.

When only yards separated the two boats he finally yelled a warning. "Give way!" he shouted. "Starboard tack!"

Possibly the skipper of the *Haulfast II* thought he could outbluff him. Luke set his jaw and held his course. And at the last possible instant Holliger bore off. The green sloop missed their rudder by inches as it crossed astern.

Marilyn's eyes were as big as saucers and her face was white. "Goodness," she laughed shakily. "Racing can be kind of scary, can't it? Were you sure we wouldn't be hit?"

"We had the right of way," Luke told her grimly. "I gambled that Mert wouldn't want to be disqualified. Maybe he's learning some sense."

Staying on the starboard tack, Luke brought the *Tern* out of Dutchman's Bay with a two-length lead. Behind Holliger, and only trailing him by a length, Bruce Canning was sailing the *Sally C* with all his usual skill.

They rounded the northern buoy in that order. Ahead of them was the long reach down the channel and past the clubhouse, and knowing there ought to be more wind away from the shelter of the island, Luke bore off to leeward.

Marilyn, hiked out on the port gunwale, had a better view forward than he. "Look!" she called out suddenly. "Somebody's in trouble—there goes the Coast Guard!"

Right ahead he saw a small rowboat overturned, with

swimmers bobbing alongside. Across the channel came the Coast Guard launch at full speed. Luke eased the helm up and let the *Tern's* bow fall off. He wanted to keep well clear of the accident and give the launch room to maneuver. The sloop lost way perceptibly as she passed twenty yards to starboard.

One of the people in the water was an elderly fisherman with his battered felt hat still clamped firmly on his head. The other was a boy of ten or twelve.

"You all right?" Luke yelled.

"Y-yeah!" sputtered the old man. "Only this here dad-blamed outboard's gone to the bottom!"

The roar of the Coast Guard boat's engine made any further conversation impossible. Luke grinned and put the helm down again, trimming the sheet. Then, as he glanced to windward, the grin vanished. Both his opponents had sailed a straight course and the detour had lost the *Tern* her lead.

"Oh, dear!" said Marilyn. "Why did they have to tip over right in front of us? Now we're behind again!"

"All right," Luke told her, "hang on to your hair and we'll see what we can do."

Closer to the wind now, the sloop was fairly flying. Foot by foot she picked up enough to pass the *Sally C* and was close at the heels of the *Haulfast II* as they went by the clubhouse dock.

Mert Holliger wasn't going to be passed if he could help it. He luffed a little, trying to pick up speed. Instead of luffing with him, Luke bore off a point or two. With ten good yards separating the two boats, he brought the *Tern's* nose up again and tried for a break-through in the lee. But Holliger was alert this time. Quickly he bore to starboard and the green sloop's blanketing cone just nipped Luke's sails in time. Once again the *Haulfast II* forged ahead.

At the south mark all three Comets were tightly bunched, but it was Holliger who rounded first. Luke followed right in his wake, staving off the rush of the *Sally C.* Then, as they started the northward reach, the wind suddenly turned puffy.

Luke took a worried look at the sky. "That's bad," he said. "If it keeps up we'll be moving in fits an' starts. Let's hope we get our share of luck!"

Every minute or two they would catch a brief gust of wind that sent them on their way. Then, for exasperating intervals, they drifted without a breeze, tossed by waves that were still running high. It was hard to keep proper steerage way on the sloop. Hard, too, to guess when the next puff was coming and be ready for it. Luke was proud of the way his crew responded. She was quick to judge the force of the wind and balance its sudden thrust. Her lack of weight made it more difficult, but in the periods of drifting their lighter boat gained a little.

There was no way to forecast the direction of those puffs. The wind seemed to shift through a full quarter of the compass—sometimes due east, sometimes southeast, occasionally almost south. Watching the surface of the water, Luke could nearly always tell a moment in advance and trim the sheet accordingly. But once, opposite the clubhouse, an unexpected gust from the rear caught him close-hauled, shook the leech of the sail and almost knocked the *Tern* on her beam ends before he could slack off.

The forward drive of that puff carried them up abreast of the green boat and a little to leeward. Mert grinned over at them mockingly.

"Don't look so scared, Marilyn," he called. "It's only water, an' you're a good swimmer. Besides, a lot o' guys'll be glad to pull you out!"

They didn't answer. Marilyn kept her rigid back turned

to the other boat, and Luke's eyes were on the bay astern. He saw the quick ruffle of a breeze coming up from the southeast and trimmed the sheet to catch it. Before Holliger woke up to the situation the *Tern* slipped through his lee and moved in front.

With the same jerky pattern of alternate puffs and calms the race went on. At the whim of the wind, sometimes one sloop, sometimes another gained a brief advantage. Canning was still very much in it. Nearing the north buoy his *Sally C* lay only a length back of the *Haulfast II*. All the other boats had dropped far astern.

Luke got to the mark first, jibed the turn and started westward. The breeze at that moment seemed to become steadier, blowing almost from the east.

"Why," said Marilyn, "it isn't puffy any more! That's going to help us, isn't it?"

Luke frowned. "Maybe," he said, "but I don't quite trust it. If I could be sure of a good steady wind I was going to try the cut. Mert probably will, anyway. Yep— there he goes! Now's the time to hope we're right an' he's wrong."

Apparently Bruce Canning had some doubts, too. He veered off from Holliger's wake and followed the *Tern* on the longer course around the marshy point. With some dismay Marilyn peered under the boom at the green *Comet*, now speeding down the cut.

"He's pulling ahead of us," she said dolefully, "and the wind's getting stronger, if anything."

It was true. But what she hadn't noticed was that it had shifted direction again. Luke trimmed the sheet. The breeze was more abeam now, coming out of the southeast. And at once the *Haulfast II* was in difficulties. They could see her slow up, her sails slatting.

"Mert was running before the wind," said Luke, more cheerfully. "Probably had his centerboard up. When that

shift came it pushed his boat over on the north bank. Look
—Johnny's trying to shove off with an oar!"

"Forgive me, Luke," the girl said. "You *were* right, but
I'll never understand how you knew."

"Just a hunch," he said, grinning. "Guess it must come
from living here on the island all my life."

They continued on a broad reach into the bay, still
leading the *Sally C,* but only by a length. The distance
grew less as they neared the marker. Canning had the
windward berth, and the nose of his sloop was even with
the *Tern's* transom. This was a buoy that must be rounded
counter-clockwise. It wasn't hard to see that Canning
meant to cut inside, forcing them wide.

Forty feet from the mark Luke jammed the helm down
and luffed. Without an overlap the older skipper couldn't
call for room—he could only luff, too, and in a hurry.

Luke had allowed just enough room to fall off again,
and he did it the instant the *Sally C* went past to windward. He brought the tiller up hard, shot by the buoy on
the right side, and came around in a tight turn, his boom
over on the starboard tack. With no chance to match the
maneuver, Canning had been forced to come about to get
back in position for the mark.

As they beat eastward out of the bay Luke could see
Holliger just nosing out of the cut. The green sloop was
no longer in contention. She was back with the pack now,
and in a way he could feel sorry for Mert. Whatever he
lacked in judgment, the skipper of the *Haulfast II* had
plenty of courage. Perhaps his valiant try deserved a
better fate.

At the moment, however, Luke had no time for sympathy. There was a tough rival at his heels—a good boat,
well sailed. Canning had brought the *Sally C* up to a
single length astern before they finished the eastward leg.

Both sloops were pointing high, both able to make the final turn without tacking, unless the wind should shift again.

For the time, at least, it was still blowing strong and steady from the southeast. Luke had the leeward berth. He was certain he could round the buoy first if he could keep Canning from establishing an overlap. But as those last seconds passed, the *Sally C's* bow continued to creep up.

More by instinct than by logic, Luke luffed a trifle, bringing the *Tern* only a yard or two away from the other Comet's course. The result surprised him. He saw his opponent falter and fall back as the wind spilled off his own sails on the lee side of the *Sally C's*, checking her forward drive.

With the marker right abeam, Luke brought the tiller up, rounding fast on the port tack. They had a two-length lead now, and they were on the last leg of the race. If there was no change in the wind he could hope to sail all the way to the finish without tacking.

He could see Marilyn's lips moving silently and her slim brown fists were clenched. He didn't disturb her, for he knew she was praying them in. That was fine. His own job, he felt, was to keep alert. He remembered the old saying that "the Lord helps those who help themselves."

Bruce Canning was too experienced a sailor to quit trying while there was still a chance. He pointed the *Sally C* high, heading up to windward. That would keep him from being blanketed and give him an opportunity—if the wind shifted easterly—to overtake the *Tern*.

Luke understood his move. He took a long look at the weather and gambled that there would be no such shift. He held his sloop on course, his body hiked out as far as possible, adding all the ballast he could to his crew's light weight. After a minute or two he stole a glance over his shoulder. He had gained another length and the breeze held steady.

"Come on, baby," he crooned to the boat, "just another quarter mile the way you're going!"

He looked at Marilyn and she gave him a quick smile, not yet of triumph but of hope. Then he looked ahead at the clubhouse dock, packed with faces, all turned in their direction. Miraculously the dock and the yellow-flagged buoys of the finish line were rushing nearer—nearer. And suddenly he knew that nothing could stop them now. They were close—they were across!

"Number three-oh-nine-five!" crackled the loudspeaker with startling volume. "Over! Great sailing, Cramer!"

Luke went on another hundred yards to give Canning room. Then he came into the wind, and as the reaction hit him he found his hand on the tiller trembling. For the last two hours, he realized, he had been as tense as a drawn bow-string.

"How about you taking her in?" he asked Marilyn with a tired grin.

*   *   *

An hour later, when the last of the scattered fleet had sailed over the line and joined the boats in the basin, there was a ceremony in the Yacht Club ballroom. Everybody was crowded around the trophy table—all the skippers and their friends and families.

Marley Evans pounded on the table with the tiller bar that served as a gavel.

"Comet sailors of the Man-o'-War fleet," he said, "I don't need to tell any of you we've got a new champion. You saw the race—some of you from a long way astern. It was well sailed, and it was sailed cleanly. Nobody, I'm sure, can be anything but proud of this teen-ager in his first season who beats such an old hand as Bruce Canning. You don't need to apologize either, Bruce. You kept him running scared from start to finish. And I expect you feel some pride in the fact you were his teacher.

"I've watched this boy, first in his own little sneakbox, then as a crew man, and now as skipper of a Comet he salvaged and refinished himself. And I say he's a credit to Man-o'-War. Let's hear a cheer for the winner of the Commodore's Cup—Luke Cramer!"

The bellow of applause shook the clubhouse as Luke was pushed forward to the table. Embarrassed, he looked at his feet, then at the giant silver cup.

"Gosh," he stammered, "it's big, isn't it? And beautiful! I never thought I'd have my name on it."

He straightened, facing the crowd. "Folks," he said, "Man-o'-War Island and the Yacht Club have been good to me. If I've learned anything about sailing it was from Mr. Canning. He's my boss, too, and I suppose I was crazy to beat him today."

The laughter died down and he went on. "But who was the first one to congratulate me? That's right—Mr. Canning. I think he'll agree with me that we both had some luck though. I don't know where Mert Holliger finished, but if the wind hadn't cheated him, up there in the cut, we'd have had a three-boat race to the line that would raise your hair."

He paused and beckoned to Marilyn. "Just one more thing I'd like to say," he told them. "My crew today had never sailed in a race before, but she had as much to do with winning as I did. How 'bout a cheer for Miss March?"

While the rafters rang again, Mert Holliger shouldered his way through the crowd. He came up to the young pair by the table and grabbed both their hands.

"Mind if I apologize?" he said, grinning. "For a lot o'

things? You're a regular guy, Luke, an' Marilyn showed good sense. You both deserved to win the Cup. But just wait till the wind isn't fluky—wait till next year!"

They laughed with him. "That's right," they said together. "Wait till next year!"